FALLING OUT OF TIME

VIKING
Published by the Penguin Group
Penguin Books Canada Ltd., 2801 John Street, Markham,
Ontario, Canada L3R 1B4
Penguin Books Ltd., 27 Wrights Lane, London W8 5TZ,
England
Viking Penguin Inc., 40 West 23rd Street, New York, New
York 10010, U.S.A.
Penguin Books Australia Ltd., Ringwood, Victoria, Australia
Penguin Books (N.Z.) Ltd., 182-190 Wairau Road, Auckland 10, New Zealand
Penguin Books Ltd, Registered Offices: Harmondsworth,
Middlesex, England

First published 1989

10 9 8 7 6 5 4 3 2 1

Copyright © O.R. Melling, 1989

Printed and bound in Canada

Canadian Cataloguing in Publication Data
Melling, O. R.
  Falling out of time
ISBN 0-670-81421-0

I. Title.

PS8576.E44T93 1988   C813'.54   C88-093000-4
PR9199.3.M44T93 1988

**American Library of Congress Cataloguing in Publication
Data:**   Falling out of time   88-40588

For Yvonne, Lorraine and Deirdre
– three mad artist-sisters –
one more against despair

Acknowledgements

Omigod a litany of "thanks to": agents John Duff and Jonathan Williams; editor Cynthia Good and all the gang at Penguin; the Whelan family with special mention of Kev who chauffeured me about; Beryl George for never-ending support; Maeve and Marcus, my gooseberry fools; Paddy and Dáithí for fun times in Clones 86; Johnny Nicholl (beloved sponsor) and Ambrose McKenna for long chats in a car; Leland Bardwell for writer's advice and a friendly cottage; and Columba, for love.

Thank you to The Canada Council for a project grant.

This book was written at Maggie's Cottage of the Tyrone Guthrie Centre, Annaghmakerrig, Eire.

1

*T*here is a twilight land where mountains rise like towers. The sky is ragged, starless, moonless. Drenched fields crawl over the hillsides. Ruins lie scattered like bones in the grasses. The first sound is the echo of rain falling on stones. Now comes the steady thrumming of a heart, a drum. It is a beat out of time, a note secreted from the crevice of dreams, a pattern begun in ages forgotten and repeated again and again in endless brooding. This country is a soft-spoken horror, a desolation of the soul; grey sky, grey stone and the masque of shadows.

They meet in this place, holding themselves stiffly in a pantomime of pride that hides deeper emotions. His head inclines towards her as he makes his greeting. The dark hair moves of its own accord like black flame. She too bows slightly in the ritual of courtesy which contains no submission. Her hair is pale and flows down her back. The rain trickles over their bodies like tears.

He looks disdainfully around him but it seems he is feigning indifference.

"Our enemies have gathered. I have seen the signs."

She follows his glance over the barren land. "Another cycle perhaps."

"Are you willing?" His tone is formal.

She smiles suddenly and the tension between them eases. The remembrance of a Golden Age flickers in their features.

"We must make it different this time," she urges.

He hears the warning behind her plea. His frown breaks the moment of cohesion.

"You anticipate war."

Even as they speak, even as their moods shift with the evening play of light and shadow, the sense is there of a vast store of memory, the wheel turning perpetually to bring them to this meeting place and the decision to face each other once again. It is difficult for them to communicate in this phase. They are too aware of the tenuous web of emotion they thread together with speech and gesture, a web so easily woven but just as easily torn asunder. A kind of torpor underlies their excitement as they reach over the ocean of the past to the possibility of another union: the state of Sisyphus approaching the summit.

"The fear of war should not stop us."

The love and sorrow in her voice catch him like fire.

"Then let it begin."

2

Deep in the forest, the air is the colour of amber. The earthen floor is matted with cones and needles. High in the treetops, the wind sifts through the weight of pine, creating a susurrus like waves coming to shore.

A woman steps through the trees. Her skin and hair are coated with a fine dust, like pollen. She puts her hand on the bole of a tree and finely-tapered fingers explore the rough surface. She stares upward to where the sun flashes in the branches, a sky-ship far away. There is a surprised angle to her limbs, a slow dreamlike movement to her eyes.

She stiffens when a high-pitched metallic sound pierces the air. With a swift unthinking motion she catches at a branch and climbs up the tree.

Beyond her spreads a breadth of mountains. She is in a forest which covers a high hill. A serpentine road winds through the trees, and speeding along the road is the source of the noise: a motorcycle heading towards her. The bike leans into curves, whirrs like the hawk dive. As it passes beneath her, she sees the slim figure astride it, black helmet glittering in the sunlight. When the bike stops at the summit, the woman climbs down and follows after it.

Michael O'Dea has parked his motorbike near the ruins of the Hell-Fire Club. He removes his helmet and smooths the bristle of red hair. He is young, hovering on the border of manhood. His face has the shy guileless look of a child, but the dark-blue eyes betray a wilful streak. Tall and angular, he moves with awkward grace through the shell of what was once a house of ill fame.

Like a prison or asylum, the architecture of the Hell-Fire Club seems intentionally grim. Squarish, humped, with windows dark and eyeless, it squats on the hill like a maleficent bird. The stone walls are grey on the outside, blackened within. The cavernous fireplaces gape like tombstones. The air is dank with the smell of badness carried through the centuries.

Michael grins to himself as thoughts of orgies and Satanic masses tickle the perverse side of his imagination. He knows the story of the great fire that burned alive the aristocratic cabal who gambled and played here. It was said that, late at night, screams still echo through the mountains.

When he saunters out of the ruins, Michael takes a cigarette from his pocket and remakes it with pieces of hashish. Smoking lazily, he eases his back against a wall. Above him glows the arc of the sky, drifting with amorphous cloud. In the distance, he can see the white monopoly houses of an urban sprawl. To his right is a patchwork scene of fields tumbling down hills. He lowers his gaze to the hill he stands upon. The coarse grass sways in the wind. The forest fringe creeps towards the summit. Dark spaces amidst the trees seem to be eyes watching him.

He breathes deeply, inhaling the scent of mountain air, damp earth and pine. The stillness and the drug work their slow magic till he is at peace. This is his favourite place, where he comes to escape the city and his life. He lets out a low sigh, a murmur of undirected love.

In the shadow of the forest, the woman is watching Michael. His face is pale beneath the fiery brush of hair. His leather pants and jacket glisten like the taut skin of a beetle. When the sigh issues from his mouth like a word, she stirs uneasily, as if in answer to his call.

Michael has noticed the worn patch of grass bounding the Hell-Fire Club. He remembers the superstition that if you run backwards three times around the ruins you will call up the Devil. Apparently a lot of people have tried it; the track is a raw wound in the ground. He decides to give it a chance.

His first run is completed with half-serious intent, long legs akimbo in backward stride. The second time around finds him grinning hugely. He has become his own spectator, contemplating the antics of a deranged self. By the third and last lap, he's laughing loudly, giddy and hiccup-ing for air.

Observing his erratic regress, the woman

can't help but laugh too. Her laughter insinuates itself into his, wells up like a song and echoes from the depths of the Hell-Fire Club.

Some part of Michael's mind finally registers the sound. He stops abruptly. Catching his breath, no longer laughing himself, he struggles to get a grip on reality. But no amount of effort dispels the pool of laughter that eddies around him, wild and unearthly and high as the wind. With frantic jerks he turns this way and that, searching vainly for the source.

He swears, in full panic now. Belief aside, he isn't ready to meet the Devil.

He makes a run for his bike.

The woman is still laughing when Michael leaves. She climbs a tree to watch his departure. Her voice trails after the drone of the bike as it speeds downhill and careers onto the grey vein of road that leads to Dublin.

3

*R*ain is falling outside. It trickles down the window, encouraging me to weep. I am roaming around the house as if I can't remember who I am. Slippers pad across the floor like an old woman and it's almost noon. I hear Damian's voice in my head – "What, you're not dressed yet?'' – that tone which makes me cringe, a child again. A child? An old woman? Neither, but I am small like a child and nurse the fears of an old woman.

I remember now the thing that haunts me, that has me wandering through the day like a misplaced person. This morning, awakening from some dream, its trails still warm between my legs, I sat on the edge of the bed, half-lost in sleep, and a string of words wound through my mind.

I wish I had a lover.

Then Damian's body shifted behind me and I was stung awake. Something's wrong here.

It's not easy to pinpoint moments of lucidity and, true to my character, I had to get the message from a dream. I'm not very bright when it comes to reality. Or maybe it's just the nature of marriage. Over the long slow days and weeks, months and years, the drift occurs insidiously, as undetectable as the movement of continents. Then comes the time when the divide makes itself known and the chasm yawns.

A tragedy is looming before me but I don't want to over-react. Calm down. Take a hot bath. It's the usual story. A woman facing the end of her marriage. That's all it is. There's no need to collapse in the ruins of your personal life. Don't die of loneliness on the way to the washroom.

The bravado cracks like an eggshell.

In the bath, knees drawn to breasts, she bleeds into the water. Veins, eyes, mouth, womb, all open and bleed. She sits in the red warmth, slides down like a pale fish, then throws back her head to cry, choking on the pain in her throat.

This country is a soft-spoken horror, a desolation of the soul.

Shivering on the bathmat, holding myself together with a towel, I am suddenly flooded with a recall of my dream. Strange that my mind should return to where Damian and I used to meet so long ago. I had almost forgotten Ireland, never mind that dark place. It had a name, to do with Hell.

A thought flickers, the first impetus to leave. I cup my hands around the idea to give it life. I could go back. The dream could be the start of something. A beginning out of an ending, as it were. I'm always trying to be philosophical.

4

*T*he bus lumbers up Buckingham Street on its way out of Dublin. Lines of washing flap from the balconies of a corporation estate. There's an old man in a wrinkled cap sitting on a bench by a low stone wall. Rows of redbrick houses line the street. Rows of red chimneypots line the sky. Now the inevitable parade of newsagents, launderettes, chemists, butchers . . . I'm not really here . . . my eyes and mind are dim with music.

The woman beside me says something and I have to remove my headphones.

"Sorry?"

She has the window seat; the twilight is glowing behind her like a halo. In her seventies or eighties, she's a tiny bird of a woman with fragile bones, wispy hair and a beak for a nose. Her eyes sparkle in a way that implies she is laughing at the world and at me. I like her immediately.

"Are you on holidays?" she asks.

"I'm going to Burdantien House, an artists' retreat in Monaghan."

"Isn't that a wonderful thing for you."

She smiles as if we are old friends.

"You're not Irish yourself?"

"I'm Canadian but I've been here before."

"And you've come back again."

"Yes."

I'm not about to elaborate with the tale of my separation. Damian in Toronto. Me in Ireland. Only Americans spill out their problems at the drop of a hat.

She doesn't seem to mind, makes no effort to probe for more. Instead she tells me about her family, scattered to the four corners of the earth, as she puts it. She and her husband are still on the farm but the land has been let out as they no longer work it. Perhaps one of her children will return some day. Her voice is cheerful and unhurried. Life is a pleasant story despite the hardship. I feel quiet and somehow comforted.

We are passing through Finglas where grey-white houses creep among petrol stations and shopping marts, and at last we are out of the city. The change is so abrupt that I sit up in my seat and stare out the window, entranced. Despite the occasional blot of house or factory, the land has risen to claim its ascendancy. This is the Ireland I dream of: silence falling over sage-green fields; hedgerows damp with mist; clouds bundled over the hills like pale hills themselves. I can almost taste the rain in the air. As the bus journeys into the heart of the countryside, I let out a low sigh.

"You love the land."

My head turns quickly to meet the old woman's scrutiny.

"I worship it," I say, surprised that I have confessed.

Is it amusement or assessment I see in her eyes? She rests her hand on my arm, talks about farming and the passage of years and something else. The healing power of the Mother Earth. I am only half listening, lulled by the softness of her voice. Her words seem to blend with the shadows of the fields that sweep past the window like wings. The sky has darkened. Night is falling. What is this story she's telling me? A "plague" of rabbits which destroyed her crops. I try to rouse myself from my stupor.

"Times like that," I murmur in sympathy, "I guess it's right to kill animals, when they threaten the livelihood of human beings."

She shakes her head as if I have missed some point she was making. Her hand gives my arm a gently admonishing squeeze.

"Why should human beings come first?"

I surface with a start. A shiver of premonition. I look down at her hand. The fingers are slender, finely-tapered, with purplish nails like shells.

Caught off guard. It's not as if I don't know these things, it's just that I keep forgetting. As I said before, I'm not too quick on the plane of reality. I need reminders, the little arrows that point to what is huge and timeless.

Recovering from my gaffe, I meet the shrewd eyes of the old woman, eyes that are laughing at me, though not unkindly.

"Why should humans come first," I agree, and we nod to each other.

5

*T*he dance at the local Orange Hall is sheer madness. We are pressed and squeezed together inside a stone building out in the middle of nowhere. The crossroads perhaps. The two-man, four-instrument band is caterwauling bad music with admirable zest. Circles of dancers spin around the floor. Shirts are unbuttoned, dresses disorderly. Faces loom before me, pink and sweaty. Energy untrammelled in such a small space turns in on itself till we are out of control, arms pumping, legs kicking, humours abandoned. We shriek as someone crashes to the ground, throwing the rest of us off balance till we teeter precariously. I expect the walls to burst asunder. This is hysterical fun. Not my idea of staid Protestantism. Another prejudice bites the dust as another "Prod" hits the floorboards.

I'm glad my partner is a big man. Like a bull in the field, he clears room around us. With a sprig of leaves tucked in his glasses, broad red face and bushy beard, he's Zeus himself towering over me. He yanks my arms to rock and roll, knocks my elbows into my face, treads on my feet with his great thumping boots. I'm too small to prevent this assault on my person and I am springing about like a puppet, helpless with laughter.

After the dance, walking the long road home to Burdantien in the company of others who are talking quietly, the hilarity of the evening ebbs away from me. My eyes wander over hill after Monaghan hill rising darkly to the sky. The road is lined with jagged black pine, an avenue of kings, and I inhale their scent with slow delight. But though I am happy and feel it and know it, still the thought manages to enter my mind, disturbing the peace like a noise.

I will never walk the night roads of Ireland with Damian again.

It's almost a year since I left him. When does the invasion of memory cease? When does the pain go away?

The road takes us past Burdantien Lake, a wide pool of light. The big house comes into sight over the swell of a dim meadow, its stone front staring over the landscape with grim elegance. Gables arch like crescent moons. Lights blink from slender windows where artists are working late into the night. Burdantien House. An artists' retreat. My latest refuge.

I will be happy here, I tell myself. I will be happy.

6

*D*anger everywhere. Shapes in the darkness, formless but menacing. I am running with Damian through a bleak grey land. Winds blow across the plain. The ground is stony and unyielding. The bare branches of trees clutch at the sky. All around us are the shadows of ruin.

We stumble, fall down, pick ourselves up, holding onto each other as we flee.

Now I see what is chasing us. Too many enemies. The ragged form of a great wolf. A serpent crawling in the grass. And above, the sharp visage of a hawk on the prey. They're drawing near. I cry out to Damian, a silent scream of fear.

We must find sanctuary.

Still weighted with sleep, I pull myself from the bed and stagger forward. Devoid of place or identity, I waver blindly on the border between reality and the nightmare I have just escaped. Then my vision clears and I remember where I am. The desk feels solid and reassuring as I grip its edges. The lamp casts a yellow glow onto my typewriter which squats like a dwarf. I light a cigarette and exhale terror.

At the window beyond, the dark presses against my room like black water. I am drowning. Drowning in a despair that seems to assault me from nowhere. I stare helplessly out at the night and know I am suffering a moment of defeat. My enemies have gathered, the wall has been breached and the darkness is flowing in to conquer me.

"Help," I whisper to the gods.

Three o'clock in the morning, the witching hour according to some, a cup of tea would be. . . I pad through the silent house like a ghost, through passages hung with faded portraits, down the carpeted stairs of the hallway, past the library and the drawing room with its great bay windows. The kitchen is dim with a solitary night-light. The long table where the artists take their evening meal together shines like a barren plain. But at the round table by the glass doors, where we have breakfast and lunch on our own time, there sits a lone young man.

"Hullo," he says. "Want some coffee? I've made a fresh pot."

His name is Michael and he has just arrived from Dublin on his motorcycle which broke down twice on the way. He's a writer. Exhausted. Arriving so late, he found the house locked up and there was nothing else to do but climb through a window. With his luck, of course it was a woman's bedroom and he frightened the life out of her as he fumbled through the dark, trying to find a door, all the time muttering his apologies.

I can't help but laugh with him at his misadventures and I regard him gratefully.

He's much younger than me. In the first seconds of our meeting, my wandering libido recognized him as a fellow traveller but I don't find him attractive. He has a flat moon face and white skin beneath the ubiquitous freckles which partner his red hair. The hair is stiff like wire, cut in a punkish style and brushed upwards from delicately pointed ears. He's like an elf, I think, suddenly paying more attention. There is an elfin quality to those dark-blue eyes which are excessively animated despite his fatigue. Staring at me with disarming interest. He is fully present, no trails of him left elsewhere in other times or with other people. He seems to own himself completely. I feel a pang of envy and admiration.

"This place is incredible, isn't it?"

He wolfs down a sandwich as he speaks, eating noisily like a child, looking around the spacious kitchen. Tiled floor, paintings on the walls, shelves of china-blue dishes, everything is arranged to be comfortable and aesthetic.

"It's paradise," I agree. "The stuff of dreams."

"How long are you here for?"

"Six weeks."

"Me too. What do you do?" he asks.

"I write fantasy."

His features brighten and he gives me a searching look. The peculiar glitter in his eyes reminds me of the old woman on the bus from Dublin but I reject the correspondence. I am not interested in this boy.

"Do you believe in magic?"

He is almost serious. I don't really want to talk about it but he's waiting for an answer. My hands rest on the white tablecloth; I look at my fingers to avoid his gaze.

"Of course I do," I finally admit.

Before the conversation can go any further, I gulp down my coffee and stand up. An uneasiness has entered the room. Something I've forgotten. A dream closing in on me? I need to escape.

"You should go to bed after the day you've had. I think I'll do some work."

"You write late at night? So do I!"

Now he stands up and the eagerness in his movement makes me frown. I want to push him away. He is tall, tall and thin, the way I like them. His body leans over my small height like a hand cupped over a flame. I can't reject this correspondence, it is so familiar. I hear an echo in my mind, Damian's voice wry and amused. *At least you're faithful to my body type.* An image is suddenly there, unasked for, unwanted, with the potency to wipe out all other thoughts. Tall black-haired Damian with great dark eyes that reflect my surrender, my doom.

"Sorry? Did I . . . ?"

Michael has caught the shadow descending over me. I feel raw and exposed. I don't know him well enough to talk. I wish I weren't in a house of strangers. The loneliness is setting in like a black wave as it always does in the wake of Damian's memory. And then the anger. I don't want to be one of the walking wounded. I don't want to carry these scars that open and bleed of their own accord. I want to be free of him. I want to be free.

The concern in Michael's face restores me to the present. My withdrawal has been too abrupt. He looks like a puppy whose nose has been slapped. He doesn't need this after a tiresome day and mishaps in the night. It was better when we were laughing, the first glimmer of friendship.

"I'm fine, really. It's just that I've been stuck at the beginning of my book and I suddenly got an idea for my musician character. You've been a help actually."

When I reach the door, I turn around to find that he's still looking at me.

"By the way, I believe in angels too."

He looks surprised, then laughs.

"See you later."

7

*T*he beginning was chaotic. A sea of sound burst into the void. Then a tune insinuated itself through the clamour, a thread of silver winding its way through disorder. The thread expands: a shining web that binds the noise to give it structure. An orb of music, smooth and symmetrical, soft as a lullaby. A sphere of order. A pearl. O.

The ideal is a mirage! A point of dissonance shivers at the centre, wells up in crescendo and explodes. Fragments of sound rain from the sky like a shower of stars.

Then silence. Silence that numbs.

But it's not over. A single note rings out. Held so long it creates multiplicity. A wire of sound stretched to span the universe. Does this sound exist outside of hearing or is it invented by the ear as it searches for sound?

Notes run along the wire, faster and faster. A current of oscillating euphony. It loops over itself, spirals with fury, strains for the limits of infinity.

The final explosion was like the beginning. A storm of sound. Then, at last, an arc of music, the composer's signature: the harmonic spectrum shattered into a tonal rainbow.

Michael stood rigid behind the metallic face of his synthesizer. Damp with sweat, the feathery skin of his costume clung to his body, except where the folds of cloth swept from his arms like wings. His red hair was gelled in cusps of flame which seemed to crackle with static. Electronic equipment towered the cavernous stage. Panels blinked eyes of light. Cables crawled over the floor. The other musicians were leaning on their instruments in postures of exhaustion. Out beyond the stage, where the dark shore of the night-club wavered in smoke, the crowd shrieked back their own form of dithyrambic madness.

Michael grinned, recognizing the results of his work. "No one should be in their bodies by the time I'm finished with them, dope or no dope." He had ended the performance with his latest and most experimental piece,

Metamorphoses. Nothing could be played after that, it said all he had to say for the moment.

He bowed before his audience, a multicoloured weave of flashing eyes and many arms. In the kaleidoscopic blur, one figure bowed back to catch his attention. Gabriel, the band's manager.

He was leaning against the bar, his greatcoat flung like a cape over massive shoulders. Gabriel the enigma. He would stand out anywhere. His large and shapely head was crowned with a fedora pulled over glossy black curls. The dark eyes, set closely together, were painted darker still with kohl. The wide mouth curled in a wolfish grin. Gabriel the tormentor. Cunning, ruthless, voraciously ambitious, in one short year he had brought Michael's genius to its fruition and he had no intentions of stopping at Dublin.

"You make it at home," he told Michael, "then you go for the real thing. America."

It was an uneasy partnership. Michael had his suspicions about Gabriel's influence and money. There seemed to be a labyrinthine network of dubious people, risky business, possibly the underworld. Nevertheless, Michael's art called for expensive equipment and large audiences. Gabriel provided these in return for a contract of control. The two had nothing in common, yet each held one half of what the other needed to fulfil his dreams. An indissoluble bond.

Uplifted by the crowd's approval, Michael forgot his antipathy and sent Gabriel a sign of triumphant solidarity. Their glances met through the phosphorous air of the club and locked for a moment like two fists clenched. Then, as always, Michael looked away. A trace of annoyance acknowledged his defeat in this little power game Gabriel loved to play but Michael shrugged it off.

Fuck him anyway.

Now something else caught Michael's eye: the glassy stare of a hawk. It was embroidered in sequins on the back of a satin jacket. Ruby eyes, blood-red wings and talons aptly perched on lace-clad buttocks. Michael followed the accipitral image and its girl host across the dance floor towards the bar.

Turn around, turn around.

At last she did, drink in hand, and he wasn't disappointed. A delicately sharp face set in a cloud of curly brown hair. Big eyes, lively and intelligent. No pretence at sophisticated ennui. She looked very happy with herself, apparently unattached. Two objects dangled from her ears and when Michael realized what they were – a knife and fork – he laughed out loud. She looked towards the stage where the band was putting away their instruments despite the cries for more. Michael waited till her eyes reached his, then he winked and made a slight gesture with his hips. He had grown used to choosing from the harem of his female audience.

Maybe she caught the harem thought, for she shot him a look of contempt and turned her back. The hawk glowered at him with dismissal.

8

I create fantasies for myself and my lover, fashion mythologies to heighten the meaning of our union. But I become lost in these designs. Entangled in my imagination. I weave spells that cloud my own eyes and blind me to the reality of the other, till I walk in a daze through a self-made world of passion. I believe in magic, in the power of the word to call form into being. Magic is dangerous. The magician is ever in peril.

It is the early hours before dawn. My desk faces the window which overlooks a grey-pale meadow and Burdantien's lake lying still as a mirror. Head bent over my words, I ignore the beauty beyond me and the first sound of birds. I ignore also the beauty of my large room: the embroidered couch and chairs, the carved bed in one corner, the paintings on the walls, the old photographs on the mantelpiece. Work-worn, hair lank, I'm wearing a baggy sweater over mismatched pyjamas and large glasses on my face.

A knock on the door. I call out, knowing it is

Michael. We have been spending a lot of time together the past week: long talks, strolls through the woods, tea breaks at all hours. Both of us are on the same schedule, working through the night and rising late in the day.

He has obviously just showered and is ready for bed, dressed in a black silk kimono that falls past his knees. His hair is wet and glistens like copper, brushed back from his forehead as if polished. I note that his features are not round but high-boned and angular and I wonder why my first impression was of a moon face. He walks towards me diffidently, a sheaf of papers in his hand. As he moves, the kimono flows around him and I catch the flash of white leg, white penis.

Is this deliberate? I am half amused, half delighted. His image is a delicious play of dark and light, but the face turned towards me seems so innocent. A sure sign of guile, I tell myself, and the moment of cynicism makes me feel old.

He sits on the couch near my desk, draws the dressing gown over his knees with unconscious modesty.

"It's good," he says, handing me the pages of my work. "Are you busy? I'd like to talk to you about it."

"Sure. Let's talk."

I can hear my own irony. I am wishing I had bathed earlier, that I was not wearing my glasses and these old pyjamas, that I might appear at this moment as attractive as he does.

The lack of synchronicity bothers me. Why didn't I foresee this? What signs have I missed?

"It hints at different elements right from the start. As far as I can tell, the story of Michael . . ." he pauses over the name, I refuse to bat an eyelid, ". . . and the strange woman in the forest is some kind of incarnation of the two gods in the valley. If this is so, why is the woman magical and not the man?"

I'm trying to pay attention to what he's saying but my thoughts and senses are wandering off in various directions. The loose shifting of his gown, the angle of his limbs, the expressions on his face are entering my blood stream with the slow stir of appetite. At the same time, I'm working my way through an idea. There are several layers to this here and now. We are two writers discussing a book. We are a male and female at the edge of sexual possibility. And there's something else. He asks why the woman is magical and not the man. Is it because I have yet to discover if the man has power? No, I mustn't confuse my story and my reality.

"The bits I've given you are a dream prologue, the meeting of the Two Magicians, the gods as you call them, and then the commencement of one of their cycles on earth. The scene at the Hell-Fire Club is to ease the fantasy into the real world. When the two lovers actually get together, they're on the same level."

Michael leans forward. His kimono opens and a smooth white belly lies before me like a plain.

"What is the book about? Where are you going with it?"

I'm overcome with an urge to explain what I'm doing as if it's important that he should know. Perhaps I want to see some recognition in his eyes. Or maybe I'm hoping to plant a seed in his fertile young brain, the first words of a spell of seduction. But do I want to weave a spell here? And what's more, is it necessary? Am I not being seduced myself by this vision in black?

"I'm writing about the kind of love that binds two people together in something larger than reality."

"Is it autobiographical?"

He asks the question without thinking and only after realizes its personal nature. A shade of pink colours his features.

My mind and emotions join at the intersection of that blush. I am touched. Caught. Say what I hadn't intended to say.

"It's based on my marriage."

Michael's eyes blink with surprise. He looks confused.

"You're married."

"*Was*," I retort, not meaning to sound so bitter.

I turn away from him and glare at my typewriter. I don't want this intimacy, this thread of gravity in the pleasant game we are playing. Anticipating the next question, I am already irked when it comes.

"Do you mind me asking how old you are?"

"I do mind. I don't see why people have to be pegged by numbers."

Sly one, he speaks of feminism and how women no longer need to hide their age.

"Are you over twenty-five?" he persists.

I remain silent but I know I'm cornered.

His eyes widen.

"Thirty?"

"Hmm."

"Thirty-plus? Not forty!"

"Piss off." I am now thoroughly annoyed. And trapped. "Thirty-three."

"You don't look anywhere near it."

"That's not the point."

"I'm twenty-three," he offers.

"You look about sixteen with those freckles."

"You're just getting me back for making you tell."

True enough. Still, he does look like a kid to me. Fresh and shining. I feel tired, old and fed up. What is he doing in my room anyway, flaunting his young body at me. Pressing his existence into my thoughts. Edging his way into my story. The cavalier self-confidence of youth, moving through the world and other people's lives with the independence of a master race.

Michael senses my withdrawal and stands up hastily, his gown a swirl of shadow.

"I'll let you get back to work."

He hovers nearby, a question mark over me.

I make a noncommittal noise and stare stubbornly at my desk. When he leaves the room, I am still looking inward, exasperated by images of long thin bodies in black kimonos.

9

*N*ight was a strange tune altogether, the after hours of Dublin City. Michael walked the streets, searching without urgency. His new piece was out there in the darkness waiting for him and he wandered to meet it.

Grafton Street meandered like a speckled snake. The bright store fronts were crisscrossed with metal shutters. Tremolos of scattered light emerging from a background? The shapes of buildings, rectangles of sound? It wouldn't be difficult to reflect this city in musical architecture, but did he want to include the human dimension? Figures moved on the jittery edge of his vision, phantoms in the anarchy of night. Some roved happily, intoxicated with laughter. Others howled in the lost world of drunkards. An unconscious body sprawled in the cave of a door. Michael turned away from some questionable thing happening in an alleyway.

Specificities, but where was the unity? He
wanted the multiperspective in his composition
but it had to pull together.

Stephen's Green lay before him. The ink-
black leaves of trees were a shawl draped over
the pavement. How could he translate that into
his own language? Configurations of sound to
recreate a city were what he sought. He wanted
to fashion with music what Joyce had wrought
in words.

He was nearing Ely Place, where he lived.
Other thoughts impinged on his creative muse.
Gabriel didn't want to invest in an Emulator.
Michael would sell his soul for one. The range of
sound it would provide, no limit! The night's gig
had gone well, the reaction to Metamorphoses
was excellent. So much for Gabriel's lecture on
"listenability," a thinly disguised order to write
something more commercial. Gabriel hadn't a
hope in hell of changing Michael's mind on that.
The dope he'd smoked earlier, good stuff. His
brain felt crisp like frost. That girl with brown
curly hair and cutlery for earrings. He laughed
to himself. Maybe Gabriel had a point, though,
and the immediate priority was the video. That
girl with brown curly hair. . .

She was walking towards him, bobbing along
the footpath with a loose happy gait. Since she
was already in his mind, it took him a minute to
accept she was real. Her high-heeled boots
clicked over the pavement. Her hair flew behind

her like wings. The sequinned jacket sparked
eyes in the night. She had seen him too, and
though he was out of costume, she obviously
recognized him.

As they approached each other, Michael
made a feint and tipped the knife which hung
from her right ear.

"How about having me for dinner?"

Her quick glance appraised the brush of red
hair, silk scarf draped loosely, long coat, slim
trousers.

He sensed her approval and grinned.

She detected the flicker of confidence and
replied drily.

"You don't look very tasty to me."

"Liar."

That made her laugh.

He was caught by the laugh and he saw that
she knew it.

Both were caught in the play of dark and
light.

"Where are you off to?" he asked, dropping
the rakish stance and using a friendly tone.

"Back to my rooms. Trinity College."

"The gates are locked by now."

"I'll go over the wall."

"My hero. Shall I walk you there?"

They were standing in front of the lighted
façade of the Shelbourne Hotel, not far from
where Michael lived, but he had lost all desire to
go home. Beneath the hotel lamps he stared into

her eyes, two points of green, wise like a cat's. He had thought at first that she was very young but when she smiled he detected the faint imprint of lines. He felt the tug of adventure.

They walked together down Kildare Street.

"My name's Michael."

"I'm Raffie," she said, "Raffie Knight," and she added automatically, "it's short for Rafael-la."

"I knew that. Do I hear an American accent there?"

"Canadian," she answered, with the tone of one who was sick of that question.

"Sorry," he said contritely.

"You're forgiven."

His eyes wandered over her. He was enjoying the long-legged stride of black stockings pulling at a narrow skirt. Glitter and lace and net. Feeding his attraction, playing his own game, he converted her into music: filigrees of sound for the stockings; a run of glissandi for the jacket; a low orgasmic hum for the tight skirt.

"What are you studying?"

"I'm not. I'm writing my thesis for a Master of Philosophy."

"You don't look like a philosopher."

"Tweeds and glasses you mean?" She made a snorting noise. "My working title is 'The Quest of the Individual Consciousness for,' " she lifted her arms grandly, " 'Oblivion.' "

"Magic."

"Everyone thinks I'm crazy except my supervisor, who's a bit weird herself. She's Irish. That's why I'm here, alien in residence, escaping the academic straitjacket of Canadian conservatism."

"That was a mouthful."

"I've been practising."

They were in sight of Trinity College. It rose above the street like a medieval town; stone walls topped with the spears of wrought iron railings. Crossing Nassau Street, they walked beneath the high balustrade.

"It's like living in a castle," Raffie said. "The Lady of Shalott in her tower." Then she murmured, *"I am half sick of shadows."*

When they arrived at the front gate, the doors were locked.

"The porter will let you in if he knows you," Michael said, thinking of past girlfriends walked to the same spot and situation.

The intimation was not lost on Raffie.

"I know. I've been late before, my dear."

Michael sensed the psychological balance which was being maintained and decided it was time to escalate. He could see she was hesitating.

"You don't really want to get in."

Raffie regarded him coolly.

"The banality of male ego."

He plunged his hands into his pockets, annoyed by the directness of her attack. That was the trouble with facing an equal, you had to keep dancing. He lost patience.

"I concede your intelligence," he said. "You don't have to hit me over the head with it."

Raffie stopped her retort before things spiralled further. She wasn't looking for a fight. Her sarcasm was as much an effort to buy time as it was a reaction to his confidence. Decisions. Decisions. Did she want to spend another Saturday night alone in her room? Or would she risk a one-night stand with this cocky boy? The humour of her predicament made her laugh out loud.

"You seem to be pretty bright yourself," she said.

Michael was already in love with her laugh. It melted the edges of his irritation and drew him back to her. He leaned forward to kiss her, a slow light kiss.

"Boy genius meets girl genius," he said softly.

Raffie frowned. There it was again. The smugness in his tone. He probably slept with a different woman after every show. Did she need this?

"And they go home together and have sex," she said sourly.

The moment of cohesion was broken. His cynicism rose to match hers.

"Why do Americans always state the obvious?"

Raffie tossed her head.

"It's a way of rejecting it."

Despite the bravado, her shoulders slumped

beneath the satin jacket and she looked unhappy.

Michael felt the dullness of defeat. They had
reached stalemate and the situation couldn't be
restructured to make it good. Silently he turned
away from her and walked back towards Grafton Street.

10

A hawk circles the night sky. Sharp eyes
pierce the infinite distance between heaven and
earth to spy the lovers.

They know they have been sighted and they
quicken their pace, stumbling through the darkness. The ground is stony and unyielding. Winds
blow across the plain. All around are the shadows of ruin. It is not easy to take flight in this
bleak land.

But already there are signs of hope. In their
path grows the flower valerian, *allheal* shedding
its white glow. And on the far horizon, the
lambent hint of dawn. Sanctuary is near.

They reach a great cairn that overlooks a
river. The passageway is dry and dark, leading
to an even darker core. Inside the house of stone
image and memory, they stand apart. Blind.
Helpless. The point of still waiting.

It happens when morning breaks through the clouds. As the solstice sun rises above the river, a stream of light enters the passageway to flood the inner chamber with the bursting of a star. At the heart of the luminous sphere the Two approach each other, murmuring their countless names.

11

"*M*ichael!"

"Raffie," he whispered, stopping at her call. He waited till the tread of high-heeled boots caught up with him.

They walked together without speaking, both too afraid to interfere with what seemed to be happening despite themselves. Threads of emotion were spinning between them, a faint web of possibility they didn't want to break yet were unready to confirm.

At one point Raffie sighed. It was a sad sound. Michael almost spoke then. He wanted to tell her he was not really an egotistical bastard and that he was basically good at heart and very interested in her as he could see she was something special. But he was afraid it would sound like so much blah blah blah and he wasn't sure anyway. He didn't trust this kind of instant attraction. It was a trap which more often than not led to disillusionment. Maybe she was right and he only wanted sex. He didn't think so. He always wanted more. The impossible, the ideal, whatever.

"How do I know you're not a psycho-killer or something?" Raffie said at last.

Michael gave her his best leer.

"Life's a risk."

She burst out laughing, a sound that thrust aside all tension in its exuberant rush.

"You have a brilliant laugh," he said.

She leaned into his body as he put his arm around her.

What was it she wouldn't say to him? She ruled her life with the independence of a queen, fortified by the power of her mind. Yet she wasn't as confident as she appeared. Always inside was the ineffable fear of conquest which made every lover a potential enemy. The danger arose only when she faced an equal, as she had discovered in the past. For that reason her lovers were usually younger than herself. This lovely Michael was another boy, though certainly talented. She had arrived late at the club, driven from the boredom of the four walls of her room, to stand shocked as she listened. Original music, complex and shattering.

A warning sounded in Raffie's mind.

"I loved what you played tonight," she said suddenly. "Who writes your music?"

Michael was aware of something behind her

question, some dark thing moving as if to wake, but he couldn't identify it. He would need time to figure her out. Like one of his compositions. The correspondence appealed to him and he was overcome with a desire to impress her, to let her know he was a match for her.

"It's my own work. I'm a composer as well as a musician."

Assuming she would be pleased, Michael was mystified by the flash of anxiety he caught in those wise green eyes.

12

She was surprised by his lovemaking. He was playful and affectionate, took his time to draw close though they were both blatantly ready before they reached the bed. His arms bound her in a circle of heat. Light kisses covered her body. She pressed her mouth to his, parted his lips, explored small sharp teeth. His breath warmed her face as he moved over her. Deft hands stroked thighs and belly. A smooth finger moved inside her with mesmeric rhythm. She caught her breath as he took her off guard. Expecting the slender finger, she received instead the finely-tapered head of the serpent, sliding in with devious ease.

13

"*T*hat was great!"

He hears the trace of surprise and his laugh is low. Smug?

"It's not age that counts."

"I couldn't agree more."

Laughter wells up. This is happiness. This is freedom.

"You have a brilliant laugh."

His arm rests on the pillow, propping up his head. The red hair stands out like exclamation points. His body stretches like a cat's.

"You're so tiny," he says. "I don't think you're quite human. You're like a sprite or something."

"I never claimed to be human."

He doesn't really hear. His face is pensive as though he is debating what he will say next.

"Why is Michael the name of your character?" He's blushing, but he presses on, determined to have this out. "And the red hair?"

It was inevitable that he would ask sooner or later but the question unsettles me nonetheless. Just before he asked it, I was regarding him fondly and thinking how pleasant it was that we were finally lovers. I was also warning myself. I know very well that one side of me can tumble him happily without complication, but the other side if woken could easily get lost and all tangled up. And here is the tangle threatening already. He thinks I'm writing about him and me. He imagines that he is the other half of the myth.

I must dispel this illusion before it can take effect.

"He was called Michael before I met you. His name relates symbolically to the other main characters. As for the hair, I can show you the notes I made last year in Canada when I got the idea for the book. Michael O'Dea, angel of light, god of fire. A redhead."

He is convinced, though disappointed, but now I am tingling with an uneasiness that promises panic. I believe in the power of the word to create reality; it is the foundation of magic. I believe in magic. Having written a red-haired Michael, here I am in bed with one! Spells are tricky things. The last one nearly destroyed me. The magician is ever in peril.

In a rush of words I explain the matter further, as if to ward off some approaching doom.

"The mythology of the Two Magicians is one I invented for my husband and myself. It was a game we played, an allegory of our love. But words have power. Did you know that "spell" means both a story and a magical formula?

"I got caught in my own myth, trapped by my imagination. I came to believe that I was truly part of an eternal couple. I'm writing out the tale to work a counter-spell. The characters are Damian and I, with different appearances. Do you see? By the time I have finished the book, what binds me to him will be broken."

Even as I speak, I sense that I'm getting my wires crossed. And within this circular explanation, a little point of dissonance sends shivers through me. Didn't the idea for the mythology come from a dream? Wasn't that how it began? My head hurts when I try to figure this out.

It doesn't help that Michael appears to understand. He should be looking at me as if I'm crazy or, better still, make some one-dimensional remark about "art as therapy." Instead it seems from his silence and the steady searching gaze that he has followed me through the words and into the spectrum of meaning. There is danger here. He cannot be equal to me. I must be imagining his empathy.

"The best cure for the old magician is a new magician," he says softly.

No! my mind screams, don't start this game again, this is not the way out!

"The best cure for the old partner is a new partner," he repeats when I show no reaction.

14

She was sleeping when he slipped carefully out of bed. A rush of affection passed through him as he looked down at her. The sheets were twisted around her body like a snake curled on the branch of a tree. In the air shimmered the scent of coupling, an echo of their night antics. He found his dressing gown and padded barefoot from the room.

Michael lived on the top floor of a Georgian house. It had an air of shabby elegance, like an old lady who has had too much to drink. The capacious rooms were graced with high ceilings and curlicued plaster as well as antique dust and time's drapery of cobwebs. Michael's own mark was one of disorder. Though he had been living there for almost a year, the place looked as if he had just moved in. The drawing room was cluttered with trunks and boxes. Piles of books spilled over the hardwood floors. Clothes dangled from couches and chairs. Adding colour and encouragement to the reign of confusion were huge canvases running rampant across the walls: lush jungles painted in lurid hue, damp and vulval with primordial innocence.

His workroom, however, was a different matter. Order had been imposed on chaos for the sake of creation. A polished piano stood in one corner. Long benches held his synthesizer, amps and tape machines. Shelves were neatly stacked with scores, thick manuscripts, books on music history, electronics and the physics of sound. A broad glass table was covered with sheets of notated paper, sharpened pencils, ink pots and pens.

Michael moved from room to room like a visitor. In the kitchen, high windows looked out on Ely Place, a narrow street, mostly offices, and quiet on the weekend. Light dappled the cupboards and counter. He turned on the coffee machine, rummaged in the bread box, laid out a tray. He would bring her breakfast in bed. He was humming to himself, grinning in his mind.

The best yet? Don't be such a bastard.

15

*M*ichael has gone back to his room. I'm remaking the bed as the sheets are tangled up. I can smell him in the blankets. It's good to have a lover again, another young one, true to my pattern. He is the seventh boy I've slept with since leaving my marriage. "A phase you go through," my divorced sister told me. "Enjoy it while it lasts." There's an edge to my grin. I admit the game I'm playing, putting numbers, people, intimacies between Damian and myself. Am I getting anywhere?

I sit in the alcove of the window which looks over the meadow and Burdantien Lake. The land is cloaked in night, invisible to me, but I know what lies out there. The minutes expand like years and still I sit.

It begins to happen before dawn. Mist and light enmesh in the air like gauze. Colours are lost in chiaroscuro. Dark shapes emerge like sentinels. Sounds reach my ears: the cry of wolves and hounds; the stamp of troops thundering over the hills; a high eerie music.

"Aural hallucination," says one part of my mind.

"Welcome," whispers another.

The presence of the Other is pervasive, moving over the landscape like a cloud descending.

I am the sash of wind that blows over the meadow, disturbing the tall grass. I am the green slope that lies content beneath the tread of cattle. I am the spine of forest that frowns over the lake at the big stone house and the tiny figure seated in the window who stares blindly back.

I am the white bird that flies over the lake. My flight is mirrored on the surface so that I move like a couple. But the golden chain is broken. My partner has fallen away from me to drown in the depths below. I see his face under the water, dark hair caught in the reeds, fea-tures bloated.

A cry echoes over the lake, the forest, the hills and the house. A cry of grief traversing the centuries.

16

Smiling a covetous smile, Michael sat on the edge of the bed and watched her eat. Her should-ers were slender, her breasts small with pink cusps. The brown hair twined and twisted like a wreath around her neck.

Raffie returned his inspection with a little grin. His face was boyish and eager, the red hair a jagged tangle over elfin features. The dark-blue eyes reflected a curious mixture of inno-cence and cunning.

The tension between them was exciting. They were intimate strangers.

"You're younger than me, you know," she said.

"Twenty-one," he answered smartly as if undergoing a necessary interrogation.

Raffie laughed.

"I'm twenty-eight."

"Ancient!" he cried, rolling his eyes and fall-ing back on the bed.

The black silk dressing gown flowed away from him as he lay at her feet. He didn't bother to cover himself and she stared at him brazenly.

"Still hungry?" he asked.

"Coming back in?" she replied.

"We'll have to talk to each other one of these days," he said as he scrambled up beside her.

They went walking in Stephen's Green, which Michael called his back garden. The cool green pond was busy with ducks. Trees dripped their branches into the water. The air was damp and warm beneath a muffled sky. They sat on a knoll under an oak tree and smoked a joint, lounging on the grass, talking and talking.

Her father was a carpenter; his was a civil servant. Their mothers were housewives. Both had siblings. She loved her family and wrote to them regularly. He was indifferent to his and rarely visited them. She had almost married, "a few things" had ended the relationship. She didn't want to elaborate. He had had a multitude of short affairs, one being described as "the ultimate catastrophe." He preferred to leave out the details as it was fairly recent. Neither was attached at the moment, so to speak.

Born and bred in Dublin, he had studied at the Royal Irish Academy of Music, then lived in Berlin for a time, playing in a punk band before he started to compose his own work. She was Canadian, born of an Irish father and Italian mother. She had spent most of her life in Toronto, except for holidays, and had worked in a variety of jobs before deciding on college. He wanted to create a new form of music and play on the stage of the world. She would be a great scholar and publish philosophical treatises. Liszt and Stockhausen were his heroes. Plato and Einstein were hers. Both thrived on city life but dreamed of being hermits in some far-off region.

"A cabin in the green forests of Vancouver Island," Raffie said.

"A stone cell on sea-washed Skellig," Michael agreed.

Each loved music and art and books and theatre. Kate Bush and David Bowie. The colour black. Weird people. Second-hand clothes. Glitter. Dope. Wine. Sex.

The wind shook the branches of the oak tree above their heads as they chanted the litany of their present lives to each other. Even as they spoke, mildly lost and elated, they sensed the leaf-thin reality of their words. Lyrated leaves floating on an older, stronger wind. They didn't need to know these things, facts which were merely the clothes they preferred to remove, but it was good to be together and hear the sound of each other's voice.

They left the park and strolled down Grafton Street. The refurbished avenue of shops and restaurants was less crowded than usual. Everyone wandered about with an aimless air. A dark-haired musician was piping forlornly in a forgotten alleyway.

"Sunday in Dublin is a small death" was Michael's comment.

"I like this city," Raffie said. "The old crouches beside the new. Too much of Toronto is cement and glass."

A pavement artist was chalking on the square in front of Trinity College. Michael rested his arm on Raffie's shoulders as they stopped to watch.

The design crawled over the footpath, snake swallowing snake in tortuous confusion. Misshapen heads convulsed. Lithe bodies contorted. The colours were cold and metallic, blue-green slithering over grey stone.

"Magic," Michael murmured.

Raffie was staring at the image as if hypnotized. Something in the aberration of form sickened her. She felt dizzy as she tried to discern where one serpent ended and the other began. Something here. A reminder. A warning. Something horrible. She pulled herself away with a jerk, away from the image and from her lover.

When Michael caught up with her, he found her shaking.

"What's wrong?"

"That thing," she managed to say between breaths.

"It's a Celtic pattern, you must have seen it before. I think the dope's getting to you. Strong stuff."

"Don't be simple," she snapped.

Michael's eyes flashed.

"Might I suggest, then, a Freudian reaction? Phallic repulsion?"

Raffie made an exasperated noise, recovered her good humour and laughed.

"You're so cute I keep forgetting you have a brain."

"Cute? I thought you said you weren't American."

17

*T*he one-night stand stretched into a multiplicity of days. They wanted to see more and more of each other, more than was possible. Michael was preparing for another concert and his new piece had to be ready for it. The first draft of Raffie's thesis was due by summer's end. They were forced to create pockets of space and time in which they could meet. Before rehearsal. After the library. Sleepless nights in his flat or her rooms. Both strained on a wire of need that only increased their desire.

One stolen Saturday they went to Howth and walked along the cliffs at the edge of the Irish Sea. It was a cool windy day. White birds glided on the air between the expanse of sky and water.

Green slopes of mountain sheered into sides of grey-blue rock. The steep path wound through gorse and stones and tufts of grass. At their journey's end was a dark little pub. Coals glowed in the grate of the fireplace. The wind rattled the windows. They sat in a corner by the fire, drinking pints of Guinness and Harp; black liquid for him, gold for her.

"How bizarre," Raffie said, looking around her. "I had a dream about this place a while ago, but I've never been here before."

Her confusion heightened her disarray. She had been unpinned and loosened by the sea winds. A high colour burned in her cheeks. Under the riot of curls, her green eyes flickered with the flames of the firelight. She looked fey, a wild creature from under water. Not quite human.

"We were here together like this," she said, "but it wasn't you and me. Well, it was, but we looked different. You know how that can happen in dreams. Your hair was dark and mine was blond. I wore a red kerchief on my head." She stopped, her eyes wide. "I was telling you about a dream! Like I'm doing right now! A different dream about two other people who were us."

"A dream in a dream in a dream," Michael said, caught by the idea.

Raffie was unnerved.

"My dad used to warn me about studying too much. He said I'd get a brain tumour."

Michael grinned as he ruffled her hair.

"I wouldn't worry about it. Sounds like you've tuned into parallel worlds."

She grew thoughtful.

"They've been proven philosophically by one of the weirder branches of quantum physics. Do you know about the Many Worlds Theory?"

Michael didn't, but he listened eagerly as she launched into an explanation.

"The thrust of the argument," she finished, "is that the universe splits – at crucial points of observer/observed interaction – into a multitude of equally real worlds. Logically the division can move forward or backward in time as well. All of the worlds correspond to what they call 'the superposition' but observers in each world are unable to perceive the other worlds."

"You're holding the superposition," Michael pointed out, "since you observed all the dreams at the same time."

"I wonder," Raffie murmured.

She stayed in his flat that night and the next day was more reluctant than usual to return to her own place.

"It's so much nicer here," she sighed. "Lots of space to roam around in. I hate living in residence, especially during the holidays."

They were sitting in the breakfast nook by the window. A newspaper lay on the table between them. With cups of coffee and pens in hand they were working the crossword puzzle.

Michael looked up from the paper to study her. Without make-up, her face was pale, childlike, exposed. She never appeared her age, even in the morning when she swore she did. He felt an ache inside. His body was still warm from their love-making and he was ready to go again. She always "tasted like more," as he had told her.

He smiled with clever honest eyes.

"You can move in if you want."

Raffie drew back.

"That's a bit fast, isn't it?"

He shrugged, kept his voice casual.

"We know who we are."

18

*T*he scene at Howth has shaken me. I wasn't prepared for so vivid a recall. The veil of time and distance has been rent to bring me face to face with Damian.

Whelehan's Pub in Howth. Coals burn in the grate. A wind blows over the Irish Sea to rattle the windows. It is a moment from the first year of our love. We have just come from a walk on the cliffs and are sitting in a corner by the fire. Damian's features, so young, so sweet, shine from the black curls of hair. The flames are reflected in his eyes like twin columns of light.

He is listening, entranced, as I tell him my dream of the Two Magicians and how we met in the valley . . .

That was the beginning of the spell which wove its way between us. In the next seven years of our lives the thread expanded: a sticky web to bind.

The circle has been drawn. Evoke an image of power.

We are in his apartment in Toronto. We have been married for several years and this is a reconciliation during one of our many separations. Damian lounges in a chair, his long body stretched out, eyes regarding me with speculation. I am sitting cross-legged on the floor by the coffee table. A single candle has been lit, throwing shadows onto the walls. Music shivers from the stereo. Though we are living apart, he has invited me for dinner and we both know I'll stay the night. He has already played me his new songs on the guitar. Songs about me. Songs about us. We have been smoking grass and drinking red wine. We are smiling at each other with lips and eyes. This is a soft time, a truce. The darkness dispelled, all wounds closed, we are happy.

My hands rest on the table, fingers splayed like a star. I look at the candle and then at him.

"We belong together, don't we?"

Damian's face glows with dark beauty. He nods slowly, leans towards me like an arrow.

"We have always been together."

"I believe that," I say, catching the intonation. The incantation.

A ritual game before bed. *Amor aeternus.* The other half of our pattern when we are not locked in enmity and battle.

The Two Magicians face each other, aware of the bodies and names they have taken in this cycle. One dark, one fair. One tall, one tiny. Both creators of words and images, artificers of myth, bound together in love and war.

Who's to say it is merely a game? Which reality is true?

"Air is my element," I say softly, moving the rite a step further.

Damian's apartment is a loft at the top of an old house in Cabbagetown. It is a summer evening, still and muggy, but no sooner have I whispered the words than a spiral of wind shakes the many windows.

We start with surprise, yet the eyes don't flinch as if *they* know.

"Air is mine," I repeat, tempting Fate, holding my breath.

Again the wind gusts in response, more fiercely this time, and a window bursts open. The air rushes into the room and snuffs out the candle.

We sit in darkness, stiff with shock. But eyes shine with amusement and assent.

"Fire is mine, my dear," Damian says, a soft-spoken warning.

The tip of the candle leaps into flame.

Did he have a lighter that I couldn't see in the darkness? Or did he use his cigarette? I won't, can't ask. Act as if you believe. The unspoken rule. And on another level, if I accuse him of sleight of hand and am proven wrong, would I not be exposing myself? To imply that the gust of wind was merely a coincidence when he hadn't resorted to a trick. The most important of the unspoken rules. Maintain the balance. If one Magician shows more power of mind, the other is in danger. I remain silent.

We bow our heads slightly, to the flicker of the candle, to the whisper of the wind. To equals two.

19

*T*wilight has fallen over the lawns of Burdantien. Wrapped in scarf and jacket, I walk through crepuscular shadow towards the lake. The barbed outline of conifer stands guard over the road. The red blossoms of the rhododendron glow like blood. Bats circle the peaks of trees. Words circle my mind. I am near the edge of the forest. My eyes are fixed on the pale promise of the water beyond.

It would be so easy. It would feel so good. To

be submerged in the depths of oblivion. To be free of this horror.

The truth. The truth. I am trapped in here. Feeding off my past, my thoughts and memories. The lady in the tower weaves what she sees in the mirror of her mind. How I long to smash the mirror, tear up the tapestry and look upon the real world. But I am bound by an ancient curse.

I am fading in this prison of the self. Muffled, vague, insubstantial, a ghost wisping its way through grey forms. Please let me out of here. I am half sick of shadows.

For all the reality I have, I might as well be a character in one of my books. God, am I? If so, that might at least convince me that I am capable of acting out a life.

No. I do not have the energy to impress myself on paper. I draw near to the lake. The promise of peace. Unable to argue any longer. Only a few words left.

I hear a sound. A rustle in the forest. A hulking shape moves through the trees. I feel weak. Too far from the house. Can't run back. Why bother. If not the lake, some other way to go.

My terror is real but I stand fast. There are no wolves in Ireland. Facts are not emotions. It is a wolf that leaps across the road in front of me, stands at the fringe of trees on the other side, and stares at me with obsidian eyes. Now it inches forward and I see, or think I see, a deep sorrow in those eyes. There are tears on my own face. I extend my hand carefully, a white flower in the dimness. The huge creature draws near, pushes its head against my fingers. A rough dry tongue rasps my skin. The eyes look into mine, filled with a knowledge that I almost recognize. Some precious thing I have forgotten.

"I'm sorry," I whisper, "but it hurts so much to remember."

I turn back from that path and walk towards the house.

20

*B*eside the little living of life are the big things: the deep ocean of dreams, the arc of the sky that is hope, the dark wind of despair. They point like arrows to a Greater Reality, one from which we came and to which we ultimately return.

Because it is beyond our experience, indefinable and only glimpsed in reflection, we can at least imagine that this Other Reality is immense, probably infinite. On the basis that it would engulf the individual consciousness, I choose to name it *oblivion*.

Ordinary reality is the ground we walk on, immediate, material and finite. Yet even as we struggle to achieve, make friends, love, procreate, we are aware of the Greater Reality that shadows us. We fear it because it is unknown but we are inexorably drawn towards it.

Mystics refer to dream and vision as the bridges which take us to this higher plane. But we can reach for oblivion in a myriad of ways: orgasm, drugs and alcohol, religious fervour, the passion of love, euphoric enjoyment of the arts. Despite differences of method or intent, the end of these experiences is the same. To transcend ordinary reality, to become oblivious to it, transported by ecstasy. *Ek stasis.* To stand outside. Getting out of one's body and, as the modern phrase goes, getting out of one's mind.

My premise is this. Consciousness separated from oblivion yearns ever to return to it. An explication of the small deaths we pursue before the Ultimate Return.

She was still typing when Michael came into the room. In a man's shirt and black stockings, she arched over her machine with the strain of concentration. As he watched her, Michael felt something tighten inside him as if those brown curls had invaded his body and were twisting around his organs.

Raffie jumped when he stooped over her and pressed his face to hers.

"That's weird," she laughed. "Your eyes don't look upside down."

"Symmetry," he said, giving her a kiss.

He righted himself and scanned the papers on her desk.

"Why don't you show me any of your work? Am I only a pretty face? Don't you respect me now that you've had your way with me?"

He had the power, the power to make her laugh.

"I'm nervous about it at the moment. This is the first stage, developing ideas along the lines of my research. I have to formulate the theory in an ordered way and argue it out like an algorithm. Right now it's chaotic, bits of thought that haven't taken their full shape."

"You're in the creative phase," Michael said. "I never thought of academics as artists."

He read the piece she had just finished.

"Brilliant. You'll have a cult following."

"That's my biggest fear. I take this stuff seriously, you know."

"Hey, so do I, but to expect the academic world to take sex and drugs seriously is asking a lot."

"That's the philosopher's job."

She leaned against him with a sigh as he massaged her back and neck.

"I'm getting a lot of work done," she murmured.

Michael glanced around the drawing room which was now Raffie's study.

"Looks like you've always been here."

She had nested quickly. Her desk held the place of honour by the window. The bookcases housed her reference works; philosophy and psychology from ancient Greeks to modern

Germans. Study notes and bibliographies lay in neat piles along the couch. On the walls, the lurid paintings circled her world of crisp paper like a whirlpool of subconscious thought.

"You can clear away the paintings if they distract you."

"I really like them. I'd love to meet the artist."

Michael grinned.

"She was the catastrophe I told you about and you couldn't meet her anyway, she's gone to New York."

Raffie laughed as she inspected the artwork with added interest. Wild eruptions of colour, a blatant attack on order and rationality.

"I bet she was a handful all right. Why are Irish people always going to the States? Everyone at Trinity wants to go there."

"It's the only place to make it."

Michael's shrug was vague and uneasy. He had yet to mention his hope for an American debut. Their love affair was in its first flush; it seemed pointless to raise the spectre of separation before it was necessary.

"Let's go to bed," he whispered in her ear.

21

Compare religious and sexual fervour. The dark mindless rites that strip away self-consciousness in the burning drive for union with the Other. Gods and lovers offer us ecstasy if we bow before them. The greater the submission, the greater the ecstasy. Compare cultic practices of debasement of the body, flagellation and mutilation with *The Story of O.*

"This is really off the wall," Raffie muttered as she typed.

She pulled the page out of her machine and turned to another piece entitled "Obsessive Love: Self-death Cloaked in Romance." She scribbled a note between the lines. *A form of psychic suicide peculiar to females?* She didn't think men suffered from this, but it could be a moot point. Depended on who had the upper hand in the love affair?

Despite Michael's enticements she had kept at her work, but the pace was telling on her. Tension gnarled her back and limbs till they screeched for relief. She looked at the door that led to his workroom.

Silence, a burst of sound, silence again.

"Are you sure it doesn't bother you?" he was always asking.

"Not a bit," she would insist. "I don't hear anything when I'm thinking."

Raffie went to the door, pen in hand, and opened it quietly.

Michael was hunched over the synthesizer. His hair stood up in spikes as he ran his fingers through it again and again. On the wall beside him was a chart marked with cubes of instrumentation – violin, flute, bass, trumpet – and the order in which he was layering them. He would play a few bars, write notes in the cube, play some more, scratch over his notes. Sighs punctuated each movement.

Seeing him like this, angular features taut, eyes blind with effort, Raffie was overcome by a desire to catch him. Capture him.

"Still want to hop into bed?"

Hands froze over the keyboard, surprised by her voice, but he didn't turn. The line of jaw remained stiff.

"Hmm."

He considered the question as if he were rolling a sweet in his mouth, but he was still far away.

"No," he decided.

A streak of rage shot through her. She couldn't stop it. Her pen flew through the air to ping off his chart like a bullet.

Michael looked up, suddenly present. And amused.

"Can't take rejection?"

"Fuck off," she said, furious at herself. Why was she acting this way? Didn't they both have the right to say no? Was she already out of control?

The anger had caught Michael and he was now regarding her seriously. The hard set of her mouth. The eyes dark with an inchoate hatred. Her intensity focused her completely so that she seemed to glitter. He changed his mind.

As they moved together into the bedroom, his hands grasped her shoulders, laying claim to her. Slivers of desire raced through Raffie to crack the glass of her anger. She untied her hair and shook out the heavy curls. He pulled his sweater over his head.

"Some people undress each other as foreplay, believe it or not."

The last splinters were in her voice.

Michael's hands paused over the zipper of his jeans and he threw her a look of impatience. Were they going to have a row about it? Wasn't he doing what she wanted? The accusations rose in his throat but his erection reminded him that he didn't want to fight. He knew how to handle her. If he made her laugh, he was in.

"Madam, your wish is my command. May I? Allow me, please."

With a great show of servility, Michael peeled off the layers of her clothing, barely disguising his haste. He could feel the laughter ripple through her. With the back of his hand he rubbed her tummy, Aladdin polishing his lamp with swift smooth strokes. When he heard her breath catch, he knew he had won.

"You'll never manage mine," he said, opening his jeans which were now uncomfortably tight.

Raffie heard the triumph in his tone, the magnanimity of the victor. With sudden fierceness she pushed him onto the bed. Naked, she arched over him, her hair falling into his face.

"I'll do it."

She pressed her lips to his, impaling him with her tongue.

A battle, Michael thought, and his desire spiralled another loop.

His traitorous body succumbed to her assault, shifting itself eagerly at the command of her fingers. She had him stripped in minutes and began working him over.

I'm losing, he conceded with a groan.

She licked the balls of his feet, parted his legs, stroked the inner thighs. Her mouth circled his penis and for a moment he thought she was going to suck the life out of him. He was going down for the count.

Not yet, he ordered himself, dredging up some pride and self-discipline. He caught her shoulders, pulled her over him.

"Round one to you," he said, teeth bared in a grin.

Raffie laughed, exultant.

The war was on.

Willing combatants, they tumbled and

fought. A no-loss situation, the victor being the one who pushed the other higher. Slippery with sweat, their bodies coiled and intertwined, tongues inserting and mouths swallowing, one beginning where the other ended. They were pinned down in turn with hard thrusts. Cries were forced from each other's throats. They drove themselves to the edge of the precipice and clutched each other over the abyss. Shouting for conquest and conquering together, they toppled into oblivion.

22

"*T*hat was great!"

Michael hummed his assent as he took a draw on the water pipe and passed it to her.

"Did you hear wings beating over your head?"

They burst out laughing.

"Let's not be cynical about this," he said, kissing the nape of her neck. "We're brilliant together, we have to admit it."

She was sitting between his legs as he tried to braid her hair. Three strands entwined to look like two. The unruly curls kept escaping him and he would have to start all over again. Their skin was warm against each other. Amidst the tangle of sheets, they sat in a cloud of body scent and hashish.

"Do you have forgetting dreams?" Raffie asked. "Sometimes I wake up in the middle of the night and stare into the darkness, overwhelmed with the sense that I've forgotten something. Something really important. Precious. A part of me."

"Sounds familiar," Michael said. He frowned as some memory attempted to intrude on the haze in his brain. It was creeping at the edges, almost reaching the shore, but not quite.

"You know what I mean?"

"It's usually about music, I think. A piece I'm supposed to write? A tune?" He hummed a few bars, shook his head, mused quietly.

Raffie puffed on the pipe, inhaling memory, courage and images till her mind was tinted with colour.

"The forgetting dream is a dream I've forgotten," she said.

"That makes a lot of sense."

They went into a fit of giggles. Michael lost track of the braid again and decided it was beyond him.

"No, no, hang on," said Raffie. She fought to string her words into a line of thought that wasn't a tautology. "There are two dreams. One is a reminder that I've forgotten something and I end up wandering around looking for it. It's a shadowy dream. The other is the something I've forgotten. It's a specific dream, a recurring one as well." She blinked. "I had it last night! The specific one, I mean. How can I keep forgetting?"

"Something else was on your mind," Michael reminded her. "You were on top of me before I woke up."

"Oh yeah," she said, laughing lazily. Then she stopped. "Funny, I don't like sex first thing in the morning. It's almost as bad as talking." She grew pensive. "Must have been the dream."

Michael waited for her to pass him the pipe, to tell him the dream.

She gave him the pipe, but did she want to give him the other? He was in it, of course. Silently she reviewed it, disturbed by the message. To relate such a thing was tantamount to revealing your secret thoughts. He would see clearly the central place he held in her reality. An admission of love, really, if the other was confident enough to read it that way. And he was and would.

"Tell me," Michael whispered in her ear, as he guessed why she was reticent.

He had abandoned the braid to relight the pipe. Raffie turned around on the bed. Cross-legged, they faced each other. The room had grown dim with the onset of dusk. Their skin was pale and cool like the moon. The smoke of the hashish spiralled in the air, an aromatic incense.

"It was you and I," she said softly. "We were

in another world. A dark dream landscape. A valley between mountains of shadow. Everything was desolate, broken, dying. The sky was grey as though a storm was approaching.

"You came from one direction and I from another. We seemed to be giants. Your hair was black and mine was fair . . . like in that other dream . . . but again, I knew it was you and I. Sort of."

Raffie took a breath.

"We were meeting each other after a long time apart."

She paused again, expecting some reaction from Michael. He stared at her without speaking, as if he knew there was more. His pupils were dilated so that the blue irises were swallowed up by the black. Dark eyes, like the man in her dream. She continued.

"We were naked and shining with light. Our behaviour was very stiff, like when you're pretending someone isn't affecting you but inside you're raging with emotion. The thing is, I knew somehow that they . . . we . . . had known each other for what felt like eternity.

"You spoke first."

"Hail, Lady," Michael said, caught up in the story.

Raffie started.

Michael saw the tic at the corners of her mouth and felt a quiver of the same paranoia. Both were suddenly on edge, wavering between fear and excitement.

"Something like that," she admitted, avoiding his look. "And I said, 'Greetings, Lord.' "

Now she did meet his eyes and she saw mirrored there her own feelings: recognition and acceptance counterpoised with disbelief and a somewhat wry amusement. It was a game. A game of words and images. A mythology rising for two lovers. They both grew calm.

"I like it. You have great dreams," Michael said. He put the pipe away, put his arms around her.

"An ancient king and queen," he whispered as he kissed her.

"Possibly," she said, moving closer.

There was something else. Ancient, yes, timeless. And powerful. She had sensed some kind of power there.

"I think they were wizards."

"Good," said Michael. "Two magicians, eternally bound together. That's what we are."

Face to face, the warm breath of the other stirred each, exposing them both. They stared and stared, fascinated. The drug was rushing through their bodies to expand the gravity of the moment till they were enveloped in a shining sphere.

"You've got stars in your eyes," Raffie said. She was trying to joke but her voice faltered.

"I love you," he said.

"Yeah," she replied, "I love you too."

23

A summer mist lingers over the lake. The odour of green rises from the grass by the water's edge. Swarms of midges spiral in the air like smoke. The wooden dock, floating on barrels, is warm and damp. The lake laps against it with slow rhythmic motion. Stretched on a towel, I'm tingling from a cold swim but the sun is a light kiss. The other women are still splashing around, three of them, a poet, a playwright and a painter. They eventually join me on the dock.

"This is the life now," says Breage, the poet.

We murmur our assent, sighing in the heat so rare for Irish weather. Though we discuss our work and our lives, the talk keeps returning to the recent national referendum. The majority of the population have voted "no" to divorce, condemning the separated of Ireland to legal oblivion. The women are angry and, as I sympathize with their plight, I silently thank the gods I married my Irishman in Canada.

I am brought back to my book, even though I've promised myself a break from it. All the memories it has unearthed of those early days when Damian and I lived together in Dublin: me studying in one room while he practised his guitar in the other; the day he tried to braid my hair, all fingers and thumbs; his voracious appetite for sex, "you always taste like more." I feel it falling over me, out of past time, an old cloak of misery that I must discard.

These other women have survived their troubles, as I gather from the talk. They are in their forties and fifties. I sneak furtive glances at their bodies. Skinfolds and soft creases. They lounge loose-limbed, comfortable with who they are. I absorb this wisdom and take hope from them.

As we stroll back to the house, I spot Michael at his motorbike in the parking lot by the painters' studios. He waves to me. The women grin when I join him.

"Speculation, speculation," Michael says, catching their grins.

My shrug is indifferent.

"I imagine everyone suspects."

"I wonder if it's against the rules."

"What?" I say, unnecessarily. Little games.

"Fucking the other tenants," he states succinctly, then laughs. "Want to come for a 'ride'?"

"Very funny."

On the bike, I tuck myself against him and my arms circle his waist. I like this closeness, this excuse to hold him in public. We maintain a physical distance out of bed, whether from shyness, secrecy or a mutual sense of independence,

I'm not sure. I love also the feel of the motorbike trapped between my legs and vibrating warmth.

We bump down the pitted avenue of Burdantien onto the smoother surface of the main road. The hills of Monaghan ripple like sea-water, field after field. A dark lash of forest opens suddenly to spaces of green like startled eyes. The high grasses at the side of the road and the blue breadth of the sky above blur together. Though we're close to the earth, it's like flying.

Michael shouts over his shoulder.

"Want to take some risks?"

He wears a black helmet, I wear a yellow one.

"Sure!" I cry, silently saying a quick prayer.

He kicks the motorcycle into higher gear and we speed madly, unseated by every bump, leaning wildly into curves. He lets out a whoop and I can't stop laughing, exhilarated by the pace and the play with death. Being with him gives me courage though I know this is ridiculous. Insane romanticism. I clutch him tighter. We'll die together in a blaze of glory.

We don't die. Nor do we crash. We come to a little village, grey and ragged like a lonely hermit in the hills. Stopping at a pub, we ask the proprietor if we can take our drinks outside. The bar stools wobble on the footpath. We set our glasses on the windowsill.

The paved street looks dirty in the sunshine.

The houses, pubs and shops creep along the road that leads through the village towards Dublin. People walk by us and nod curtly, suspicious of strangers acting strangely.

Michael leans his shoulder against the pub wall and drinks from his pint of beer. One foot rests on the rung of his own stool, the other stretches lazily to claim mine. A young colossus straddling two worlds.

"Don't you drink at all?" he asks, eyeing my glass of orange.

When I shake my head, he looks surprised.

"Did you ever?"

"Once upon a time. I don't use drugs or alcohol any more." I look over the rooftops of the bleak village to where the rise of hills swells like a timeless ocean, a larger reality. "Imagination is enough of a bridge to get me where I want to go."

"Your characters are doing a lot of drinking and drugging."

"Their enemies are gathering."

"Rather trite, don't you think?"

I'm irked by his criticism, but it's really the memories that are upsetting me. They crowd my mind like dark angels.

"Drink and drugs had a lot to do with the destruction of Damian and myself." The statement is made flatly to end the subject. "I liked the story you gave me."

He is all attention, eager, shy.

My first glimpse at his work. "Liked" isn't

the right word, "intrigued" would be more appropriate. A strange tale, written as a transcript of tapes stolen from a psychiatric hospital. It works three levels simultaneously, telling of spies, sex and heroin addiction. The central symbol is triplicated, the gun being weapon, penis and needle. He likes to play with multiple dimensions. A coincidence?

As Michael talks of art, I watch him closely, this confident and intelligent young man. I am forever being misled by his appearance, the shock of red hair, the freckles, the childlike enthusiasm. Already I suspect the man behind the boyish pose and I wonder at the reason for his mask. Something here all right. Something dangerous? I mustn't make more of him than what he is, but then again, what is he?

He's chatting away about structuralism and post-structuralism. I'm surprised by his knowledge. It's as if I'm determined not to recognize him as an equal, even though he often says things which are important to me.

"We create our own reality," I say. "What you believe can influence what happens to you. I view my life through a veil of mythology. This is how I know the world and therefore this is what my world reflects."

Mischief flashes in those dark-blue eyes which regard me with sudden intuition.

"What about 'cognitive dissonance'? What if you are totally misreading the situation?"

All the unsaids that go between the lines of conversation. All the undercurrents that may or may not be there. Is he warning me? Or is he playing catch-me-can-you? Or are we simply two writers discussing theories of reality. Do the extra dimensions exist or do I imagine them because I want them to be there?

My grin matches his.

"In case of error, I rewrite the script."

As we laugh, warm with sunshine in that grey little village with the green hills beyond, I feel a lightness which I can't identify at first. Then I name it, still laughing. This is new bliss, this moment, this complication.

24

*H*is body is as lively as his mind and has a will of its own. The range of odours is varied and strong. Potent. Even after a shower I can smell him on my fingers and recall the cloud of scent that rises from him in bed. He doesn't like it himself. He climbs in beside me, sniffs under the blankets.

"Do you smell feet?"

He lifts his arms and pokes his nose under them.

"Jesus, I showered this morning."

"I like it," I tell him and he looks at me as if I'm mad.

I am. Fast becoming. Besotted.

25

*B*ut sometimes when this red-haired boy strains and stiffens above me, he seems suddenly older. And the shadow of long dark curls falls over my eyes.

26

*H*e has volunteered to do some work in the garden at the back of the house and I, the faithful sidekick, have trotted out to help him. Spades dig into the earth and turn over the soil which the poet Kavanagh sang about. *The stony* *grey soil of Monaghan.* We delve the tumbled rows for bedding vegetables, hot and sweaty from our labours.

"How long were you married?"

His face is averted, choosing not to see if I'm bothered by the question.

"Seven years."

He stops to think. Returns to his digging.

"The difference in age between Michael and Raffie."

His quickness puts me on edge.

"The number is significant in other ways. It's a symbol of power in some numerologies."

Michael nods. "Usually allied with three."

"The difference in age between Damian and me."

It came out before I could stop myself. (I don't like it when the web tightens like this.)

"Seven and three makes ten," Michael mutters. He's digging faster now. "The difference in our ages."

"Pure coincidence."

There are some patterns I refuse to recognize. Nor am I about to point out that he is my seventh lover since . . . He's already hot on the trail of his own hunt.

"Are you three years younger or older than Damian?"

"Older."

The word snaps out. My limbs are trembling. We shouldn't be working in this heat, I'm being overcome. Spots float in front of my eyes. Who is this man tormenting me? Who is this man tormenting?

"Why did you leave him?"

The spade plunges into the earth. One foot pushes down to drive it deeper. A foot rests on a slender neck to keep a face to the ground. Where is this anger coming from? These words?

"There was a honeymoon period before we got down to the real business of tearing each other apart. Great love and then great pain. Terrible things happened over the years with all the drinking and drugging, but that wasn't the only reason it failed.

"Something changed without me noticing. Something died. Or perhaps what I thought was there was only an illusion fed by the drink and drugs. I don't know. When I search through the ruins of my marriage, I'm like an archaeologist trying to extrapolate a culture from the bones and shards of a midden heap.

"In the end, by the end, I knew I couldn't stay with him. He didn't believe in magic any more and without his cloak, he was merely . . . a tyrant."

A foot rests on a slender neck to keep a face to the ground.

Where are these tears coming from? Not my eyes. I don't even know where I am. Everything is blurred and shining with light. I see a face. Red hair aflame. Is this brightness his or is it the sun? Somewhere in the haze I grow aware of a hand on my arm. Fingers press gently into skin.

"I think we've been digging this hole long enough."

The statement pulls me back to earth.

"Yeah," I agree, laughing a little madly. "The King is dead."

27

An image of the King. A house in Toronto. One of the early years of our marriage. A Canadian winter blows outside the windows. Snow spirals like powdered glass. The room is soft with dusk. Wood burns in the white mouth of the fireplace and red shadows dance on the walls. Damian sits on the highbacked couch, a wine-coloured dressing gown draped over his shoulders like a mantle. His hair is black as the night, his eyes darkly shining. I kneel between his legs. My lips move over his smooth belly. My head bows before him, overcome with awe, conquered utterly, a slave to love.

28

*M*aking love is a divine escape. To lose oneself in sweet oblivion. Blessed oblivion. His body is so familiar to me. Like Damian's. Expel the thought. Long. Lean. Firm legs. Strong arms. And the same wildness. The same? Head thrown back, body arched like a taut bow, breath and sound whistle through clenched teeth. Eyes turn inward. Lost.

His hand lies between my thighs. One finger delves gently, indolently, in and out.

"Are you doing more work in the garden tomorrow?"

"What?"

"I was thinking of furrows."

He laughs, kisses me.

Both our minds move back to the garden.

"Why do you think he stopped believing in magic?"

"I don't really know. It could have been the move to Canada. I told you he was Irish, didn't I? We met in Dublin when I was studying at Trinity. Perhaps Toronto killed that part of him. It's not a magical city. Or marriage might have done it. Maybe he just grew out of it. He was very young when we met."

29

A month after I met Damian, he brought me to his parents' home in County Kerry. His father was a civil servant who had taken early retirement to become a "gentleman farmer." They had a big country house, the kind I always imagined: whitewashed walls, a hallway of dark wood, marble fireplaces, a separate room for books. We had. to sleep apart but that didn't matter. We were in the first flush of love, sex was only part of the shining orb that surrounded us.

We went on long walks through the fields and woods and though I know it sounds hopelessly romantic, the truth is the countryside looked more exquisite then than I can ever remember it. Everything had a glittery edge, like the landscape of a dream. Everything was perfect.

He brought me to a lake hidden in the hills behind the house. Holding my hand, he took shorter steps to match his stride with mine. A long-legged young man, black curls falling to his shoulders, great dark eyes, his beauty always startled me like some rare creature. And I was a slight girl with long blond hair. Damian was twenty-one; I was three years older.

We crossed the streaked grasses, climbed

through hedgerows, inhaled the wet air. The lake lay in a comfortable hollow of hills, but it was neither comfortable nor placid itself. The water tossed restlessly against the wild reeds and rushes. A grey mist shimmered over the surface like a cloak.

"Burdantien."

Damian's eyes were lost and musing as he said the name in Irish.

"It means 'burnt light'."

Bordering the lake was a spinney of tangled trees. This was his favourite place, he told me, and I knew it was an offering.

The spinney was like a green chapel to some old nameless faith. The branches of the trees twined together to form arches above our heads. The pattern of leaves and light was like stained glass. A sprinkling of white hawthorn, "faery lace," he whispered to me. And all the miniatures underfoot: brown pods spilling their seeds like stars; threads of spider web; beads of lichen. Water trickled in tiny streams. Tintinnabulation. Earth chimes.

Damian crouched beneath a holly bush. Dark eyes watched me, a secret smile. I knew I was being judged, not by him but by the things he believed in. I moved carefully in that sacred place. My smallness allowed me to explore without disturbing the delicate symmetry. I found it resting on a stone and carried it back to him cupped in my hands: three feathers bound with strands of hair, dark and fair.

"Three is the magic number," he said.

And he smiled at me with so much love that I brimmed over, unable to speak.

It was a game we were playing, was it not? Two young lovers weaving a spell.

30

*T*he land is a wild damp garden of spring. They have been journeying through it for a good while. Speckled cloaks fall from their shoulders as they walk hand in hand. Sometimes they sing, other times they play games of chase, shape-shifting into many guises. Now skyborne among the clouds, white birds linked by a golden chain. Now racing over the hills with the speed of four-legged creatures.

They stop by a shining lake. She lights a fire on the shore while he wades into the water to fish. Their laughter echoes through the quiet. When they have finished their meal, they lie together in the warm grasses.

They know they are being watched. The shadow of the hawk's wing passes overhead. They glimpse the grey blur of a wolf in the trees. They see the soft track of the serpent on the earth.

Holding each other, they inspire courage with breath.

"We have power."

"We will not be defeated."

But they must move on. Their enemies are near.

31

"You're late," Gabriel said as soon as Michael entered the hall.

The others were already on stage, tuning their instruments, arranging the equipment.

"So I am," Michael replied.

His arm was around Raffie and he tightened his grip as Gabriel frowned at her.

"No women at rehearsals. That's our policy."

Raffie's face flushed. She wasn't easily intimidated by men and she had been warned about Gabriel. Nevertheless, his undisguised hostility, coupled with his appearance, alarmed her. He was over six feet tall with a heavy-set body that exuded power and the intimation of violence. Despite the broadness of frame, his face had an elegant vulpine slant accentuated by dark hungry eyes and a crown of black curls. In his late thirties, Raffie guessed. She could feel the force of his personality trained on her, searching for clues of strength or weakness, scrutinizing her stance, her clothes, her relationship to Michael. She couldn't speak.

"That's your policy not mine," Michael said coldly. "She's my guest and she's staying."

The animosity between the men seemed to darken the air around them as will matched will.

Raffie was surprised by Michael's calm and felt a pang of pride when the other backed down. With a contemptuous shrug Gabriel left them, shouting to one of the band members to fetch him a coffee.

"Okay?" Michael said to Raffie.

"It's a party," she replied drily. "You'd better get to work."

Raffie moved to the back of the club and sat among the empty tables and chairs. She should have stayed at home, she told herself, she'd be at the concert, there was no need to attend the rehearsal. A disturbing thought: did she have to be with Michael all the time? The spectre of her growing dependence made her feel vulnerable and prey to Gabriel's periodic glares in her direction. She wanted to shrink, to make herself invisible.

The musician who went for coffee had included Raffie in the round and he brought a cup over to her. The gesture broke her discomfort. She smiled gratefully at the tall awkward lad with thin hair falling into his eyes. He blushed and looked away. This would be Luce, the youngest member of the band. Michael had spoken of him. At seventeen he was already a professional, a prodigy on wind instruments. Yet his face had a bruised inward look, the mark of something lost. It was Michael's belief that he was on the needle though Luce denied it.

"I don't want any bloody junkies fucking up my music," Michael had fretted to Raffie. "If there's one thing that could pull us down before we get up, it's that. I've told them again and again, dope's okay and any kind of sex but no goddamn junk."

As she watched Luce return to the stage, Raffie suspected that Michael was right. There was definitely something wrong with the boy. His movements were distant and irresolute. He seemed to be floating in his own little bubble. While the others bantered among themselves, Luce stood without speaking, staring at the silver flute in his hand.

Before the rehearsal got fully under way, Michael would grin or wink at Raffie but eventually his attention turned completely to his work. He distributed sheets of music, explaining and exhorting.

"Something different, lads. Tachismo not machismo."

Looking from the outside in, Raffie could see how he operated. The master musician blended control with freedom, threading his will through the desires and abilities of the others. She thought to herself, does he direct our relationship with covert power? Is he the master magician? She tried to imagine what would happen if one of the band chose to rebel but there was no sign or hint of that possibility. Their acquiescence was evident as they asked questions, nodded eagerly, laughed at half-joking commands. And he, sovereign lord of his musical world, was gone from her. To a realm where he ruled absolutely.

Raffie nursed a moment of fantasy. She would like to be a member of Michael's band, happily submitting to his benign dictatorship. But she couldn't hold the image. It didn't ring true. She would be the point of dissonance that didn't exist in the group, the renegade with her own ideas on how the piece should be played. Reassured by this affirmation of her character, Raffie returned to herself. She was not a hopeless case trotting after Michael like a slave. She had brought her work with her. Taking papers from her handbag, she spread them on the table and began to make notes.

What is the motive behind the search for oblivion? Again and again these experiences are sought, physical ecstasy through union with the lover, spiritual ecstasy through union with the divine. What is being sought ultimately is loss of consciousness, one's own annihilation. To lose one's self in sweet oblivion. Blessed oblivion.

Raffie was still writing when she grew aware that Gabriel was standing behind her. Caught up in the flow of thought, she didn't acknowledge his presence or interrupt what she was doing. He sat down beside her, leaned towards the page. She sensed by his sudden stillness that he was surprised and intrigued. Pride in her work rose to give her strength of mind. She had just finished *blessed oblivion* when she decided to add *eyes and eyes and eyes.*

Without looking up, Raffie waited. When she heard the sharp almost imperceptible intake of breath, she wondered for a moment if she had been wise. Then Gabriel laughed. It was more like a bark than a laugh and it made her jump. She was pleased, though she tried not to be. Her reactions to him were completely ambivalent. She considered him dangerous, brutish, didn't want him near her, and yet and yet . . . she liked a challenge.

Suppressing a nervous laugh, she turned to face him. His eyes were heavy-lidded and hypnotic but devoid of hostility. He took a packet of Turkish cigarettes from his pocket and offered her one. She took the black and gold stick with as much grace as she could muster. His movements were deliberately slow as if he were prolonging time to the point of a scream. He lit her cigarette, held her gaze through the spiral of smoke. She refused to break contact. A slight nod of his head granted her tenacity. She didn't relax, sensing that this was a ploy to put her at ease and then catch her. She didn't like power games but she could play them if she had to. Determined not to speak first, she smoked in silence.

Gabriel's wry smile seemed to concede her decision. He sat back, stretched his long body like a cat, and blew smoke rings in the air. They drifted into each other.

"I don't like women at rehearsals."

His voice was low and measured.

"I don't like the boys to get too involved. My reasons are simple. The girls they tend to pick up are losers, out for sex and drugs, money and excitement. Hoping to hitch their wagons to a star. That kind of woman is bad news for a serious artist. Too much of a distraction. You need concentration, tunnel vision, singleminded purpose to make it big. Unfocused genius goes nowhere. Ends up on the slag heap with all the other might-have-beens."

He didn't direct his words at her but looked upwards as he continued to blow rings. In spite of herself, Raffie warmed to this subtle courtesy. He was giving her the freedom to listen and react without his surveillance. She also felt a nudge of respect. What he was saying made sense to her. And she heard as well some form of apology – no, that was too strong a word – rather an explanation for his earlier behaviour and now a dispensation for her as someone different. Or was she imagining all this? She didn't think so. She doubted he said or did anything without multiple motives.

"Tell me what you are doing. Are you a philosopher or a psychologist?"

So adroit he was. He didn't call her a student. So sinister this flattery. She was succumbing even though she knew she was succumbing. What harm could come from sharing her ideas with him? She was not deluding herself that he was interested. His eyes were two black points trained solely on her.

As Raffie detailed her theory, she watched Gabriel's features shift and change. Her words obviously triggered something in his mind which affected him deeply. He had cast aside the veneer of control as if it were merely a social formality no longer required.

"Do you separate dark and light forms of oblivion? Malign versus benign paths to self-annihilation?"

He used her terms of reference with ease, he spoke her language. And his intensity made her shiver. A tremor of fear? Or attraction? She knew what he was insinuating.

"You talk about sex and the famous *petite mort* of orgasm." He spread his long fingers on the table and regarded them thoughtfully. "Sex can be played by puppies and they lose themselves in harmless antics. The word is 'fun.' When two tigers mate, they claw each other in an orgy of mutual destruction. Love with knives.

"As for drugs, a joint will transport you into an affable state of non-being. It is the needle that pours a river of fire through your veins, burns your mind and soul till you are a black streak on the wall, a holocaust victim blasted into oblivion.

"Benign paths are but a shadow of the darker ways which are pure and thorough. The ideal aspect is . . . " Gabriel smiled, almost apologetically, "evil."

Raffie nodded slowly, spellbound by his logic. She was not unmindful of this possibility secreted within her theory. The worm at the heart of her philosophy. The death wish. But evil? Was that the ideal? The true path? She wasn't sure and yet she was drawn to the notion, drawn to Gabriel. She began to ask questions.

Lost in the discussion, Raffie didn't notice Michael looking over at her from the stage, a frown on his face, music forgotten for the moment.

Michael saw his lover lean towards Gabriel, her brown curls falling over pensive features. Against the black gloss of hair, Gabriel's face was white and narrow, with eyes half-closed, poised to strike.

32

*M*usic surged from the speakers, an eerie discordant sound. A dark whisper stirred. Something entered the room. Passed through the celebrants. *What is it, childe?*

Michael and Raffie's flat was crowded with a noisy flamboyant group of actors, artists, writers, musicians. It was a costume party. Masked beings and strange creatures tincted the rooms like a Brueghel panorama. Everyone talked, laughed, drank, smoked. Drugs were shared with casual intimacy. The tone was unreal, dreams and nightmares roamed among the revellers, hallucinations mingled with surreality.

In black gowns and speckled cloaks, the hosts of the party moved through the throng like eels in a pool. With faces powdered white, eyes whorled with kohl, Michael and Raffie charmed their friends. The ideal couple. A romance of pentacles and silk, confidence and beauty.

Gabriel's entrance was well timed. Midnight. When the party was at its peak. His image broke the confluence of the gathering as everyone stopped to stare. A hulking figure, he wore a mask that tore at the light heart of their play. It covered his head like a hood, the bone-white feathers knit as finely as skin. Below two red orbs of eyes, a hooked beak clawed the air. The great falconiform head peered down from god-like heights. The Egyptian Horus. *Hur.* The hawk.

Michael was standing near the stereo.

"Fucking magic!" he cried and made a sweeping bow with his cloak.

Laughter looped around the room. The party spiralled up another notch.

Raffie brought Gabriel a glass of red wine. He looked at her costume and then over at Michael's.

"We're magicians," she said. "The First Two."

He nodded as if to grant her wish but the movement seemed dangerous, the beak too close.

"More power to you," he said with a sharp laugh.

She waited to see if he would remove his mask to drink, but he tipped back his head as he lifted the glass. The beak opened like pincers and the wine poured down his throat, a flow of blood. Raffie suffered the sensation that he wasn't disguised, then flashed him a grin of admiration.

Michael called out to Raffie as Bowie's *Heroes* welled up from the stereo. She met him at the centre of the floor and they danced together, matching move for move. Witnessed by the approving eyes of their audience, a public rite of unison.

As the hours passed, the party waned to a dimmer phase. People sat or reclined, voices murmured, here and there couples entwined, reflections of the First Two.

It was Raffie who noticed that Gabriel had disappeared. She drifted from room to room seeking him out, as if his absence created a lack in her. Unable to find him, she came to the last possible place. She had declared the bedroom out of bounds, but she knew already that he was in there. Gabriel who obeyed no laws, certainly not those set up by people he considered beneath him. She doubted that he would even consider the law applicable to him. Gabriel, the eternal exception.

She was tingling as she put her hand on the doorknob. What might he be doing in this inner sanctum? Did she want to know? Did she have the right to intrude? Anger followed her rush of anxiety. It was her bedroom. Intoxicated with wine and dope and curiosity, hungry with some other feeling she couldn't name, Raffie turned the handle and opened the door.

Gabriel was at the edge of the bed. One knee leaned on the mattress as he stooped over, arched like a bow, still masked. The stern visage of the hawk pointed downwards. The hooked beak seemed about to plunge into the slim body sprawled below.

Luce looked even paler than usual. His eyes were half-closed, fixed on some unknown paradise. The sleeve of his shirt was rolled up, the white flesh exposed. Above the elbow, a black band lay limp, like a poisonous snake that has slaked its thirst. And the bite of the snake was evident on the soft blue crook of arm. A tiny drop of blood.

Gabriel, the dark angel, needle still in hand, was leaning over Luce in a possessive posture. The master with his favourite slave. The murderer with his beloved victim.

Something deep in Raffie's psyche was wakened by the hellish beauty of the tableau. Though she could have wept for Luce, though she shook with a rage that incited her to attack Gabriel, at the same time, at the same time she felt a quiver of excitement and the clenched fist of ache in her womb.

Her sharp intake of breath expressed all – horror, disgust, grief, fury – but it was also the inbreath of the first thrust.

Gabriel heard the sound and with mesmeric slowness turned to face her. Through the mask of the predator he appraised her flushed features, the glitter in her eyes. He saw. He knew.

Neither spoke as their looks met over Luce's body. They were far above him, birds of prey circling the sky over the carrion of life.

Raffie was approaching the edge of a precipice she had never come to before. She wanted to draw closer, peer into the abyss. She wanted to know the unknown, what Gabriel was feeling in this moment of power. This moment of evil.

Slowly, too slowly, he dropped the needle onto the bed, a discarded weapon, and two white hands, the murderer's hands, lifted the mask. Against the fall of black curls those honed features, as pale as his victim's, shone with beatific rapture.

And now the full lips parted in a smile which included her in his conspiracy of love.

Raffie was gripped with terror. Of Gabriel. Of herself.

"No," she whispered.

It was a weak negation and she knew it.

Gabriel's smile thinned to a gash that shattered the illusion of sweetness. As if tiring of the game, he shrugged impatiently. The jerking motion broke the bond between them which seemed to emanate from his body like a sticky thread.

Raffie drew back, released and shaken. She closed the door behind her but not before she heard the hiss of a word.

Soon.

33

*I*t was much later, when everyone had gone home, that Raffie told Michael what she had seen. They stood among the ruins of the party, spilled ashtrays, discarded costume parapher- nalia, the remnants of food and drink. The stereo was still playing, bagpipes wailing over an aban- doned battlefield.

Michael was furious.

"Shooting him up? In our bedroom? The fuck- ing bastard! Luce is just a kid! What the hell is he trying to do? Wreck the band?"

They were both high, unstrung. The sudden quiet after the party and the pervasive disorder left them shaky and displaced.

"Our enemies are gathering," Raffie whis- pered.

"What? What did you say?"

Raffie shook her head. She felt cold. A name- less fear was seeping through her. Michael looked wan and distracted. *Weak.* The word crept into her thoughts unbidden. She consid- ered it with surprise and glanced at Michael to see if he was aware of her disloyalty. But he was not attuned to her as he ranted against Gabriel, repeating old arguments and grievances. The synchronicity of the evening had been broken. Anger clouded Raffie: anger at the break, at Michael, at her judgment of him. And some- where in the mist, her attraction to Gabriel crawled to the shore of her mind and dug long fingers into the sand.

"Have you ever used a needle?"

The question caught Michael off guard. An odd sheepish look crossed his face.

"Yeah, a few times. Gabriel . . . "

He blushed at the admission, at its implications, and added quickly, "He doesn't have that kind of power over me any more. That's why we fight so much. If he wasn't such a good manager I'd fuck him out altogether."

The brave words didn't convince Raffie. Her judgment was confirmed. She saw Michael as an insubordinate serf shouting hollow rancour against a king. Her anger grew. She wanted to hit him. If he was weaker than Gabriel, how could he be equal to her?

"Would you shoot me up?" she demanded.

Michael was confused, shy, as he sensed her offer of submission. His eyes pleaded with her.

"Don't do this, Raf."

Her rage burst then, a wild flood of emotion and images which included Luce's spent body and her own overwhelming desire to be in the same position. Even if she begged for it, Michael wouldn't exercise that power. The memory of Gabriel leaning over the bed taunted her. He would do it gladly, she knew, and her body ached at the thought.

"You are fucking useless," she said.

Michael's features crumbled before her contempt, enraging her further. She could have killed him. She opened her mouth to insult him again but he walked out of the room. She heard the bedroom door slam and the lock turn.

Left at the centre of her fury, Raffie boiled to the point of madness. She ran over to the stereo.

The needle screeched across the record as she tore it from the turntable and flung it against the wall. The disc exploded in a rain of black fragments.

She stood still, shattered herself. She had just destroyed her favourite album, a small but precious part of her. What was she doing? What was wrong with her?

Alone in the ruins of the party, she could see shadows of herself and Michael dancing together at the heart of their friends. The King and Queen. Two charming magicians. A bubble of happiness, burst by her own hand. Despair filled the vacuum left by her rage. Dully she stared out the window at the dark of night. Against the glass, moths were battering their soft wings in vain.

34

*T*he room is obscure with shadow. I am at the edge of the bed. The mattress gives way beneath me as I rest my knee upon it. Michael seems far below, spread-eagled, blankets tossed aside. A fair-skinned boy, naked, innocent. The angle of his limbs is one of helplessness and prostration but I know he is a willing victim. I can't see him clearly unless I turn my head to the side, this way or that. As I gaze down at him, I feel tenderness and desire. Why is there an iron taste of blood in my mouth? I reach out to touch him but stop when I catch sight of my hands. Curved claws. Deadly talons. If I touch him, I'll tear the delicate fabric of his body. Now I am aware of the form I have taken. Blue-black feathers coat me like a pelt. My eyes peer over a short hooked beak. If I kiss him, I'll slash him to shreds. I don't want to hurt him but my need is unappeasable. I want to consume him. Pierce his flesh to the bone, enter the organs and eat the heart. Total penetration. My beloved's body taken into mine. Mine. Mine.

A thunderous beating of wings. I swoop down.

35

*R*affie woke up screaming. She was on the sofa with Michael's coat over her. And Michael was there, crouched beside her, red hair and young face rumpled with sleep. His arms held her as she wept.

"I don't want to hurt you."

"I know. I know."

36

*W*e are sitting in the kitchen, at the round table near the glass doors that lead to a rock garden and a little pool. Michael is reading a science magazine as he drinks his coffee with noisy slurps. I am watching the sky. It's a grey luminous day. Light is diffracted through muffled clouds to display what Damian used to call "the god effect." The weather has been changing continually, one day sunny, the next miserable. Like my humours. I steal a glance at Michael. Like his behaviour towards me. When I joined him for lunch he looked up briefly, frowned as if I had brought something to the table he hadn't ordered, then returned to his reading. How can he be so indifferent? So casual? More important, why oh why can't I?

Fuck him anyway.

I begin to review the past few weeks of our relationship, trying to sort out fact from fiction. During the courtship period, before we went to bed, he was excessively attentive, almost servile, bowing to me in manner and speech. Then came the night of the kimono, his first overt move in the mating dance. We started sleeping together shortly after that and the steps took on a faster pace and more intricate pattern. Long drives through the countryside. Long sessions of lovemaking. Long conversations in bed. And suddenly this week, without reason or warning, I am flat on my face. Out in the cold. I'm not hurt (who am I kidding?) but dismayed and surprised. It has come too abruptly. *Coitus interruptus.* What signs did I miss? Am I so out of tune on this plane that I have misread everything?

I consider what I know of him from talk and observation. Despite the boyish appearance, his background includes hard drugs and a wide range of experience. At times he expresses a kind of cold cynicism that borders on cruelty. However, when I commented on his inclination towards the dark side of life, he replied earnestly that he was as easily seduced by benign things. (Am I benign?) Like me, like so many I have known, he is a Narnian exile who has wandered through the world looking for magic. That incident he described to me: lost in a green wood one day, he was overcome by the awareness of Pan striding over him, a goat-legged colossus.

As for his work, it shows scattered genius, the product of a high intellect but unfocused as yet. Nor does it reflect the whole of his personality. The pieces I have read are negative and misanthropic. They show nothing of his lighter aspects.

His lifestyle? He subsists in Dublin like a street urchin, an "urban fox" as he calls himself.

Constantly on the move, books and baggage packed on his bike, he lives off his talents and instinct.

Off women?

This last thought creeps into my mind unbidden and I view it with perplexity. A random notion.

Perhaps he lives off women.

Financially? Emotionally? Ah yes. Lights blink on. Conclusions whirr into place. We've got him. Type: the charming philanderer. Ruthless. Heartless. Literary model: Nicholas in *The Magus*, a predator who feeds on the emotions of women.

That makes sense.

It also makes me a potential victim if I don't keep control. Of him. Of myself. I contemplate my position. (That's one of his phrases.) I'm the older and, with any luck, wiser player at this game. Tried hand that I am, I should be able to outmatch him.

Next question. Do I want this character?

Varied pictures come to mind. There are times when he is not attractive, a raggedy-arsed youth shuffling ahead of me in mismatched socks and untidy clothes. Sitting in the pub, he bores me with stories of school days not as far behind as mine. The red hair and freckles, the hint of roundness in his features, are hardly my vision of male beauty for which Damian is the archetype.

And yet, there are other times when these

images are upset. Dressed for a night out in suit jacket and wide trousers, silk scarf draped around his neck, he appears suddenly thin and mature. The dark-blue eyes, quick as his wit, train the intricacies of his mind solely on me. Then the red-haired boy shines with force and appeal.

As for this brusque withdrawal, regardless of other emotions, it challenges my pride. A gauntlet flung down. I will not be cast aside. I am the one who does the leaving.

That is precisely the moment when I decided to weave words around him.

Pouring myself another cup of tea, I smile over at Michael and speak casually.

"I'm going to work another level into the book. I'm going to write about you and me."

The veil of indifference is rent. He looks up quickly, eyes riveted on my face.

I lean over the stream with baited hook, peer at the creature I am about to . . .

"Meta-fiction!" he says, caught by the idea. "What's the gist of it?"

I'm overcome with the killing urge. My mouth is dry.

"The cynical view would be a woman writer bemoaning the loss of her husband while fucking a boy and somehow working it all into a fantasy."

He recoils from the jab. I imagine a little choking sound. But I see something else. A hardening behind the eyes, wily, knowing.

"What's the ideal view?" he says evenly.

Touché. My admiration for his parry melts the anger, the will to hurt.

"Something more," I admit. "Another cycle of love and magic."

He smiles slowly, his face brightening as accord is reached.

"You'll have three layers, then. Writers, heroes and gods."

"Fantasy, fiction and reality."

"Can I help you with the plot?"

Of course I answer, "Of course." And of course he already has. Meta-meta-fiction. The word creates reality. The foundation of magic. But I am uneasy. As always when a spell gets under way, I find myself wondering *who* is being magicked?

37

One foot holds the door open as Michael enters the room, balancing a tray with teapot, cups and milk jug.

"Don't move, I'll do everything," he says when I remain at my desk.

We've been working all afternoon. He sets the tray beside me, pours the tea with a great show of servility, then returns to the couch where he has been lounging. His long legs dangle like loose threads. His face is relaxed, friendly, mischievous.

"Is Gabriel based on your husband?"

"That's hardly fair. Damian was a lot of things but he wasn't evil."

"I wouldn't say Gabriel is either."

"No, you wouldn't, would you." I glance at him in a moment of doubt. "I don't know where he came from. He just walked into the book and took over."

Michael looks away. I've noticed that lately, the shifting eyes, the inability at times to face me directly. What degree of duplicity does the boyish mask hide?

"And I've already told you. Raffie and Michael correspond to Damian and me."

He isn't convinced. His mouth has a sulky twist.

"There seems to be a certain amount of inversion going on."

In more ways than one, I think to myself, but I counter his point.

"A mirror image is reversed but it shows the same thing. Can we get back to the notes?"

Michael has agreed to tell me his love history to help me with the male writer character. My motives as usual are multiple. Indeed I want the information for my book, but I also want it for myself, to learn about his relationships with other women in order to understand his relationship with me. Is he aware of the dual nature of

the situation? Or is it, for him, merely a matter
of ego, an audience for his exploits, a sexual game? On the other hand, I may be mis-
judging him. We are friends as well as lovers
and he is willing to help me with my work. Why
can't I accept that? Because it exposes my own
duplicity?

His first powerful memory belongs to age
thirteen. A summer in Kerry. One day he caught
a glimpse of a woman in a car. She had a
moon-like face and long black hair. Day and
night he thought of her, a romance devoid of sex
but fired by an intense adolescent urge. Weeks
after, he was stumbling over the bogs, looking
for the car and the dark-haired woman. He knew
he wouldn't find her but still he searched and
hoped.

That seems to have established his pattern.
Seeking an ideal which he knows can't possibly
exist. The mystical crossed with the carnal as
his quest resulted in unmitigated promiscuity.
He makes a sincere effort to calculate the number of his lovers. Becomes lost in countless
memories and one-night stands. Has the grace to
blush when he realizes it is a herculean task.
Finally confesses, in fact, that it's impossible.

"Never mind sex," I say, amused at his dis-
comfiture, "tell me about love."

Only a few in this category. He can name
them and as he does, his face flickers with
warmth or darkens with pain. He explains that
love instils in him an intensity of desire which

becomes an overpowering need for more and more. An obsession. An addiction. A hunger that cannot be satisfied. Sex only fuels the intensity and hence the hunger.

"When the extreme is not there, what do you have then?"

My question is put cautiously. Sadly I recognize that he doesn't evince this extremity of feeling for me. Why sad? I don't have it for him either. He is describing what I felt for Damian.

"Affection is different from love," he replies shyly, no doubt aware of the ulterior motive. "It's hedonistic, pleasurable. I like to give pleasure as well as receive it."

I nearly laughed. That's the same line my last boy used, "I like to give pleasure." Do they learn it at school or what?

"How does the love obsession affect your life?" I ask.

My thoughts turn to the lethargy I suffered, the difficulties functioning as a separate being, fading in relation to Damian's strength of will.

"Incredible energy," Michael says. "Explosive. The adoration is to the point of disturbance – hate and fear – but it spills out in excess drive that fires every other activity. There's a feeling of expansion, my self erupting into the universe."

The face on the other side of the coin. The antipode of the same pathology. It's as if the male-female love unit were a manic-depressive one. The man flies into the burning orb of the sun: the woman plunges into catatonia.

Now he is describing the relationship which almost destroyed him. I sense Damian's presence in the room as the words evoke . . .

Fantastic heights and terrible depths. A lot of drink and drugs. Going mad together. Burning down the world. Both wanted to own the other completely. An insanity which was devastating but irresistible. Each tried to break the other, break from the other. Fights grew to wars. Sitting on the edge of the bed, head in hands, thinking Berlin? New York? Paris? Escape. Where? But whenever one was about to leave, the other would panic, change tactics, be nice.

"How?"

Why do I bother to ask. I already know.

Michael shrugs. His face crumples.

"Show affection. Cook a meal. Make promises."

The slump of his shoulders, the hurt in his eyes, makes me want to go over and hold him. But I can't. It's not me he's mourning.

The memories have collected. A dark compression wedges into my heart with brutal force. Rage and grief inextricably imbedded.

"Yes, I remember. Once it was so bad we stopped talking and just held onto each other, knowing that if we spoke it would start all over again, the horrible stuff we couldn't control. So we said nothing. Lay together for hours, clinging to each other for dear life. Jesus."

Why am I crying? It ended a year ago, how

can I still feel this? But even as Michael felt it, so do I. What that girl was to him, Damian was for me. Blind passion, love and obsession, pain, life. He entered my world and changed it utterly, dismantled and rebuilt it with himself as the cornerstone. He was the one who went with the word *forever*. I've wept for him, bled for him. My heart I gave him, my mind, my soul. No one else will ever get as much, I swear it.

I wipe at the tears angrily, ignore Michael's look of sympathy, and return to my work.

"That's the cycle, isn't it?"

My tone is matter-of-fact, Ms Anna Lytical.

"First the Golden Age, when the two lovers shine with every possibility and potential. The mystery of the other is boundless. Contemplating the beloved is enough to send you into a state of bliss. The ideal is present, descends over the two, a shining sphere of harmony. The best of each is unfurled like cloths of gold. Everything that corresponds is accented. Each is the complement of the other and the prophecy is fulfilled.

"Then comes War. As inevitably as night follows day, darkness light. What is woven together must be torn asunder. The best, having been shared and consumed, calls forth the worst in its wake. Dissimilarities, dissonance and antipathy. In a trial by fire, the lovers are driven to bare to each other all that is dark, hateful, most difficult and deep within them. No one is perfect. Illusion gives way to disillusionment, order to chaos, love to hate.

"Finally, in due course, Separation. The great divorce between heaven and hell."

"Are you describing your mythology?"

"I'm describing my reality. What difference does it make? All lovers fail in the end."

"A cynic's view."

"What's the alternative, 'they lived happily ever after'? That's a fairy tale. Marriage and children are simply a slower and, if you ask me, more torturous form of love's death. I prefer the blaze of glory myself."

"So all incarnations of the First Two are doomed. That means Raffie and Michael will break up."

"It's inherent to the spell. They will fail even as my husband and I did."

Even as you and I will.

38

*T*hree days later I face the realization of my words. If I hadn't had that conversation with him, would this incident have occurred? But it's pure egotism to think you are the prime mover of everything that happens to you. If not egotism, then solipsism. Wasn't it inevitable, whether I said it or not, that he would show his darker side, the one I always suspected. And perhaps if he has this urge to hurt me – but what a rationalization! – it means that there is more between us. Stupid rationalization. Dangerous.

We are sitting in the drawing room, at the table in the alcove of the bay windows. The other artists have gone to bed after a late-night party of songs and laughter. The mad old poet who was playing the piano kept stopping to demand, "Does Ireland exist? Or is it a dream?"

It is near dawn. Dark clings to the windows with the last grip of night. Michael has been drinking all evening. Whiskey, my eternal enemy, that golden-faced drink which distorts familiar features to those of the Stranger who can possess the bodies of drunkards. Loki, Lord of Evil Mischief.

He is sitting opposite me with a look of sly speculation, as if contemplating the damage he is about to inflict and how far he will go. There is a dark cast to his face; his eyes have a tint of red. He does not look attractive to me in this guise, yet I don't leave. Am I caught?

He takes a cigarette from his packet without offering me one. I lean forward and help myself.

"Bitch," he says coolly. "I've only a few."

He throws the lighter at me.

A jolt of surprise and anger, but not really surprise. I have seen this face before. I have been in this place before. And even as I recognize the scene, I have to ask myself how it is that I choose this type of man. I don't believe in coincidence. Patterns are repeated *ad infinitum* if one does not move to break them.

I don't move. I stay to be hurt some more, spellbound by the repetition, paralyzed by the question why. This should happen to me. Again.

Words issue from his mouth like poisonous mist. Swirl around me. Something about my writing. His voice is strained with contempt.

"You talk about 'readability.' I would call it 'marketability'. "

An old wound opens and bleeds slowly. Damian's lips twisting with scorn. *You sit at home all day and do nothing. You'll never publish.*

Michael's eyes, darker than I have ever seen them, stare through me, gauging the effectiveness of his weapon. I sense a hunger here, the smell of blood, the exercise of power.

"People like to mix people up in their fantasies."

And what else? What else?

"Do you really think your work could be wedded with mine?"

Wedded? Webs of weddings and beddings. Wedding writers. Bedding writers. What a waste of paper, of fucking and of fucking time.

I leave before he finishes his tirade. The words aren't important anyway, only the fact that I have been attacked and from a quarter where I wasn't expecting it. Caught off guard.

Missing the signs again. But there was no profession of love, so why should its corollary, hate, come into play? Or have I been wandering in one of my dazes? What was the spell I worked on him? To catch. You don't bother catching something unless you really want it. Was I falling in love with him under the illusion that I wasn't? Is that what he guessed? Is that why?

I walk out of the drawing room, out of the big house and down the grey steps that mark another tombstone in my bizarre attempts to find a partner, a match. I cross the path where the rhododendron drip their hearts over a veil of leaves. On the periphery of my vision, Burdantien Lake exhales the burnt light of dawn. And beyond the lake rise the hills of Ireland, enduring beauty, ever-promising. Infinite possibilities or infinite lies?

I am shaking. A red-haired boy. I can't be in love with him. It's too soon after Damian. Then how could his attack have so much effect? I feel as if I've been torn to shreds. The wind is blowing through my ribboned self. Why didn't I fight back? Where did he get this power over me? And while I'm at it, why is he as much a part of my book as Damian? The worst cure for the old obsession is a new obsession. I know that. What on earth, what in hell have I been up to?

I weave fantasies around myself and my lover, create mythologies to heighten the meaning of our union. But I become lost in my own designs, entangled in my imagination. Blinded

*to the reality of the other, I walk in a daze
through a self-made world of passion.*

The road turns down to the lake but I don't
follow it. Instead, I step from the path and into
the woods. The trees are slender giants who
reproach me with sighs. I walk among them,
seeking answers in the secret language of my
Mother. Tongues of ivy twine the limbs of conifer. Where the morning light breaks through
cloud and branch, it sparkles on the dew like
tears of the sun. The air is tinted green in all its
shades: silver-pale, bright lime, forest black. I sit
on a stump and find myself surrounded by
cone-droppings, the brown vellum of last sea-
son's leaves, wild weed and flower. All around
me, the trees whisper warning.

Unsafe. Unssssafe.

39

She lies asleep in his arms. He touches her
gently so as not to wake her. Searching out the
worst of her wounds, he places a hand upon
them to heal. She forbade him to do this before
she slept – they need their power to fight the
enemy – but though it might weaken him, he
can't bear to see her suffer.

A fire burns at the mouth of the dolmen. It

casts a red sheen over the great stones that shelter them like a tomb. Beyond the walls, in the cold winds of night, the circle of oak trees whispers warning. They have strayed into the wastelands where their enemies rule. The sacred rath can protect them for only a little while.

He bends over her. A hopeless, shielding gesture. The flames of the fire reveal the gashes on her body, the anguish in his eyes.

"Why must it be this way? Why can it not be done differently?"

40

She woke late and wandered groggily into the kitchen. Michael was sitting at the table, legs crossed, head bent over the newspaper. His plate showed the ruins of toast and marmalade. Raffie glanced over at him, then frowned at the pile of dishes that spilled into the sink.

"Someone will have to wash up one of these days," she said as she rinsed a few.

"Hmm," Michael agreed, without looking up. "I couldn't even find my mug."

The accusations hung in the air, needing a third person to settle on and, failing to find one, clung instead to the two accusers like a prickly skin. The day had nowhere to go but down.

Raffie slammed the cupboard doors as she made her breakfast.

"The racket in here," Michael muttered.

She threw him a glare and he beat a hasty retreat to his workroom.

Raffie ate her meal alone and without enthusiasm. She recognized the humour she had woken to, but that knowledge brought little release. There was a dark compression inside her straining to burst out. A black boil of discontent that trickled into her arms and spine till she felt weak with the ache of despair. She was helpless before these sporadic depressions. They came from nowhere. Had she inhaled something? Bog air? Poison?

It was an arbitrary descent from joy, as though the heart of her life were beating elsewhere. A tree swayed on another plane by winds she knew nothing about. If she wasn't the arbiter, the prime mover of her own state of being, then who or what was?

She struggled for a perspective. What was her life? Working on the Master's thesis, hanging around with Michael, working on her thesis, sleeping with Michael. She saw herself moving round and round a delineated sphere whose perimeter was steadily shrinking to a dot. Her dad's joke about philosophy: "a cat racing in decreasing circles till it disappears up its own arsehole." Was that where she was going?

No, that wasn't the whole picture. She often felt that some impossible ideal overshadowed her existence, crossing at times with the here and now to make itself known. Then the breath of the world would catch in her throat, a cry of wonder. What times were these? Making love, doing a good drug, listening to music . . . the things she listed in her theory.

A different motive behind the desire for oblivion? Not a death wish but a longing for the Perfect?

Raffie's mood only worsened with these speculations. She didn't want to think about philosophy. She didn't want to be trapped in her thoughts. She wanted to *live*.

Go for a walk maybe? Too lonely. Get Michael to drive her somewhere? He was working. She could hear the synthesizer emitting squeaks and honks. She went into her study, sat down at her desk, stared at her papers. Pointless garbage. Motes of light sailed in front of her eyes. A whirring sound rang in her ears. She wanted to scream. A sentence wormed its way through her mind unattached to any sensible image.

Our enemies are near.

Michael's machine was blasting cacophonous sound. It drummed through her brain till she twitched. Unable to bear it any longer, she went to the door that separated their rooms and pulled it open.

Hunched over the keyboard, Michael was playing madly in a paroxysm of escape. He too was in a foul mood and, like Raffie, didn't know why. If he had stopped to analyse the situation, he might have noted that Gabriel's absence on a business trip had robbed him of his usual outlet for aggression.

"I can't work with that noise," Raffie said in a voice loud enough to be heard.

Michael stopped abruptly. His head jerked up like a dog on the hunt. He didn't look at her.

"That noise is music."

A pause.

"And more important than your rubbish."

Now he did turn around, and the scorn in his dark-blue eyes chilled her as much as his words. She faltered under his judgment. How did he know she was defenceless at that very point in time? That she herself considered her work worthless?

Michael saw the crack in her confidence, the pale flesh waiting to be pierced. A surge of memory unearthed what he had buried, what he thought he had forgiven and forgotten, the night she attacked him. It was his turn. Unbalanced by bad humour, justification in place, he couldn't resist the killing urge. He wielded the weapon she seemed to have put in his hand.

"You're just messing about. It's something to keep you busy. You'll never publish."

The cut went deep. And his own success was shield as well as weapon. His work was flourishing; he had followers, reviews, a manager's dreams for him. What did she have but high grades at school and the support of one professor?

Raffie crumbled under the plausible truth of his blow, found herself unable to retaliate. Her eyes stung. She saw him through a veil of tears. There was no trace of love or remorse in his features. Pitiless, the face of her intimate enemy triumphant.

"You bastard," she whispered.

She ran into the hallway, threw on her coat and slammed the door behind her.

With a satisfied grimace, Michael returned to his work. He fiddled listlessly with potentiometers. Ran his fingers through his hair. Glared at the algorithms above the keyboard. It was impossible. All wrong. Why had he done that? The emptiness in the flat weighed down on him. The silence echoed loss. Raffie's image hovered in his mind's eye, the collapse of her features, the tears, the hurt.

"Damn," he said and switched off his synthesizer.

41

A red-haired boy. Does he mean that much to me? Or is it that I need so badly to love and be loved in order to convince myself I am real.

In the laundry room, I'm doing my wash when Michael comes up to chat, his puppy self,

loose-bodied, all smiles. I stare at him with angry
eyes.

"You have a short memory."

"What?!"

The smile disappears from his face. Tense,
anxious, he stares back at me.

"Don't you remember last night?"

How does he manage to look cornered and
mystified at the same time? Two personalities?
Excellent camouflage. The left hand knows
naught.

I am already forgiving him. I can hear my
mind whirring into rationalizations, selectively
forgetting, whitewashing feelings till they are
faded images flickering across a screen from
years ago.

"You were really obnoxious, you know."

As I remind him of what happened, repeat his
words, I am fascinated by the shock I see in his
face. What reality is this? Am I speaking to the
right person? Have I got the right story?

"O God," he says. "I woke up this morning
and knew something was wrong. But not you, of
all people."

Yes. Me. Of all people.

"Will you accept an apology?"

"That's not the point."

But already I am drifting, back into the daze,
the spell, the fantasy . . .

42

*M*ichael grabbed his jacket and the two hel-
mets that hung like a couple on the hall stand.
He took the stairs in double leaps and ran into
the street. No sign of her. He unlocked his
motorcycle, wheeled from Ely Place onto Hume,
then drove around the square of Stephen's
Green. Where was she? His mind raced wildly as
he sped in and out of traffic. When he stopped at
the Harcourt Street lights for the second time, he
forced himself to think logically. She was probably planning to leave him. Where would she go?
She was practical, made decisions quickly, might
even be arranging at that very moment to move
out. Where could she go?

By the time the lights changed, he knew.
Steering his bike past the Green, he headed
down Dawson Street towards Trinity College. He
found her in the porter's lodge filling out a form
for her room. She glared at him as he touched
her arm tentatively.

"Fuck off," she said without hesitation. "I'll
collect my things later."

"Let's talk about it. Come on, we'll go for a
drink."

"I don't want to drink."

Her voice was flat and unyielding. All her anger blazed in her eyes.

Michael glanced at the porter who was pretending not to listen, though his grey beard twitched like a rabbit sniffing a good scene.

"A coffee then," Michael persisted.

He was beginning to panic. Her mind was obviously made up. He could feel her strength of will like a great wall between them. And not a twinge of retreat in those green eyes, hard as beryl. How could you hate someone you were supposed to love? But he knew. He knew.

She was handing the form to the porter, taking out her wallet. The man gave Michael a slight shrug of sympathy.

This was it, Michael realized. All or nothing. She was moving out of his realm, beyond his influence. He was losing her. The blood rose in his face and burned through his skin till he beamed a fiery colour to match his hair.

"FOR FUCK'S SAKE I'M SORRY!"

He roared it out, astonishing both the porter and Raffie as he fired his last volley against the wall.

"Jaysus," the porter muttered admiringly. All pretence at indifference fled and he stood back to view the outcome.

Raffie was stunned by the assault but the breach had been made. Amusement flickered in her eyes. There was the merest hint of a grin at the corners of her mouth. The hand that held the wallet paused.

Michael knew he was on precarious ground, could blow the whole thing if he didn't follow up strategically. Erasing any hope of victory from his voice (she would detect it instantly, he knew) he continued to plead in quieter tones.

"I'm a shite. A wanker. You can beat me if you want. But please please talk to me about it. Look, I'm in bits. I'm making an unholy show of myself. What else can I do to prove I'm sorry?"

She was trying not to laugh, trying so hard not to give in. He gave her his best stricken look, his little-boy-lost look, his absolutely-devastated-and-at-her-mercy-and-in-her-hands look. He was not only over the wall, he was in the citadel.

Kneeling at the feet of the Queen, he searched for ways to graciously cloak her surrender. If you lift the siege, Milady, I will not destroy your city. Believe me. Trust me.

As they left the porter's lodge together, Michael caught the thumbs up signal from the older man and was thankful that Raffie hadn't.

When they reached the motorcycle, he handed her the yellow helmet. Gloom was settling over her in the wake of her capitulation. She seemed pale and fragile, pitiable. He was distressed that he had brought her to this.

"Back to the flat?" she asked dully.

"We'll go for a drive," he suggested.

He leaned over her with kindness and attention, wanting so much to make it up to her, to wipe away the bad feeling.

"Into the mountains. Remember that place I told you about?"

Her face brightened at the offer and she smiled at him. Michael's heart tightened with the sadness of love. As he kissed her, they clung to each other with relief.

They drove south through the city. The press of Raffie's body against him, the vibration of the bike between his legs were familiar sensations which reassured Michael that all was well in his world again. Safe. For a while at least.

As they approached the Rathfarnham Golf Club, something equally familiar but less reassuring appeared on the scene. A tall figure stepped from an airport limousine, black fedora tipped at an angle, snakeskin boots to match his briefcase.

The two of them saw Gabriel just as he spotted them, but when Michael reduced speed Raffie leaned forward and called in his ear.

"Keep going!"

Laughing like naughty children, they sped past the manager with a shout and a wave. Both caught the look he sent them. Not anger but a cold devious grin which seemed to give warning.

You'll pay for that, my dears.

They headed down Whitechurch Road, through Tilbradden and Rockbrook, towards Kilakee. The Dublin mountains rolled around them like the humped backs of dozing animals.

Stone walls and grey-skinned trees flanked the road. They turned into a car park that bit into a forested hill and Michael walked the bike past the stanchions that blocked their way. A narrow track spiralled up the hill like a serpent round a staff. Jagged pine shadowed them on each side, the sharp perfume cutting the air. As they neared the top, the ground levelled out and the bike bumped onto a grassy summit.

The ruins of the Hell-Fire Club crouched in front of them like a gaunt bird of prey. It looked haunted, a house of stone image and ill-famed memory.

Raffie shuddered as Michael led her inside.

"It's creepy," she whispered.

"The original name was Montpelier House," he told her. "It was a hunting lodge and they say it was cursed even before the Hell-Fire Club took over because it was built on an ancient tomb.

"Then in the eighteenth-century a clique of rich young rakes bought the place and used it for gambling, orgies and black masses. There's a story about a man who accused another of cheating. When he looked under the table for the fallen card, he saw that his adversary had a cloven hoof."

Raffie shivered.

"How come you know so much about it?"

"Haven't you guessed?"

He loomed over her.

"Stop it!"

They leaned out the cave of a window. Michael pointed to the worn patch of grass below.

"If you run backwards three times around the club, you'll see the Devil."

"Really? Have you tried it?"

Michael frowned as something tugged at the back of his mind but Raffie had moved on to another thought.

"Does Gabriel come up here?"

"Why do you ask?"

"It suits him somehow, I figured he might." She had caught the edge in Michael's voice and decided to change the subject again.

"Have you ever fucked here?"

Michael's eyes lit up.

"You pervert."

He drew her away from the window and pressed her against the wall. Hands slipped under her sweater as he kissed her.

Raffie was already regretting the idea but Michael had taken off his jacket to warm the stone floor. Impatient with her slowness, he pulled her down beside him, opening her clothing and his. Their flesh seemed sickly white in the dark. The stale air caught in her throat. But when Michael moved inside her, the hard thrusts incited her desire to match his.

Half lost in a swoon, Raffie felt a cold shadow fall. It wasn't Michael who pushed so forcefully into her but a black-haired man. She cried out against him.

43

*R*econciliation is a dance step in the mating rite. It pushes the relationship into another loop so that the cycle is repeated in an upward or downward spiral.

Photographs, in the mind's eye, of Michael and me:

A towel is draped over my shoulders as I sit straight in the chair. He is behind me with comb and scissors.

"Watch my precious ears!"

"Rather pointy, aren't they?"

In the drawing room, I stand at the bay windows and watch the twilight dim the grasses. Rooks circle the copper beech and its companion oak. A sadness cloaks me. I'm helpless before these sporadic depressions. Michael pokes his head around the door, walks over to me, ruffles my hair.

"Not in good form today?"

He brings me to his room and shows me a dream he has recorded.

"I am in a house. There are two people sitting in rockers on the veranda. I'm related to them somehow. They talk quietly about a vague danger drawing near. I get more and more anxious. From a distance, a figure approaches the house. Someone carrying a gun. When it gets closer, I see she's a woman. Is she coming to kill us? At first she seems older but the more I look at her the younger she appears. I am attracted to her. She lies on the ground in front of me, toys with the weapon in her hand.

" 'Relax,' she says. 'This will take a while.'

"Then a shimmery haze comes over her and I know she is turning into my ideal."

Needless to say, I think it's a great dream.

I'm sitting cross-legged on the floor and because I feel cold, Michael has wrapped a blanket around me. He brings out pieces of his work and chats exuberantly, obviously trying to cheer me up. That alone heartens me. Now his imitation of an Irish dancer, poker-faced and legs bandy, makes me screech with laughter.

"You have a brilliant laugh."

Later, I hand him back his blanket and say good night. He waves towards his bed almost casually.

"You can pop in here if you want."

Another day I knock on his door, put my head in and find him sitting motionless at his typewriter.

"I'm working like a madwoman. Do you want to take a tea break in a little while?"

When he turns towards me, his face looks distracted and unhappy.

"Sure," he says dully.

I close the door, open it again a moment later.

"Are you all right?"

His features loosen, some cloud leaves him and he smiles.

"Yeah, I am. Thanks. Come and get me when you're ready."

That night in bed, his arms around me, he kisses my forehead.

"When you came back today and asked me how I felt . . . I was thinking what an awful place the world was. No magic."

Ensconced in the library, under low-hanging lamps, we pore over a master chart to plot the stories in my book.

"The Hell-Fire Club must be important to you to put it in twice."

"Damian and I used to go there a lot."

"It's one of my favourite spots too. I meant to tell you that. I was up there the day before I came here."

"Really?"

Shivers of coincidence. Synchronicity. Delight.

O to fall in love and never fall out again.

He carries a helmet under each arm.

"Want to go for a ride?"

44

A sunny day. Ideal for a drive in the countryside. The road twisted and turned, rose and
descended, riding the waves of a vast green sea.
Blackbirds sang on the telephone wires. Cattle
dotted the fields, motionless as standing stones.
Again and again that special site would appear,
a circle of oak trees cresting a high hill. The
faery raths that sprinkle Ireland like stars.

Speeding freely, the motorcycle would over-
take tractors lumbering along the road or the
occasional lorry belching exhaust. But for long
stretches of time there was little evidence of
mankind. The villages and towns were tucked
away in crooks and hollows, like Eve under the
arm of the Sistine god. Humans were the least of
creatures in the great presence of the land.

They came to a village and stopped for a
drink. The pub was empty, dim like a church on
weekdays. Wooden stools lined the counter. Gro-
ceries and sweets mingled with bottles of whiskey. Brown bags of spuds leaned against the
beer barrels.

Raffie glanced at the sunlight that crept
through dusty windows to scatter yellow motes
in the air.

"Can we take our drinks outside?" she asked the proprietor.

The short plump woman was startled by the request, but she heard the "American" accent and smiled indulgently.

"You'd want to enjoy it while it's there," she agreed. "It's seldom enough we get the sun."

They brought their stools out onto the pavement and set their drinks on the window sill, giggling to each other as people stared at them curiously.

"This is the life," said Michael as he rested his back against the pub wall.

His hair was afire in the sunshine, his face young and happy. Raffie smiled at him over the rim of her glass. He leaned forward and tipped the gold cross that hung from her ear.

"Nice. You should paint it black."

"I wouldn't do that," she said indignantly. "I'm not into Satanism."

Michael raised an eyebrow.

"I heard you talking about it with Gabriel last night. You sounded interested to me."

Raffie shifted uneasily. Gabriel had been telling her more about the Hell-Fire Club, his dark eyes transfixing her as he related stories of devil worship and unspeakable practices in the style of Gilles de Rais and the Marquis de Sade.

"He's helping me with my theory," she said lamely. "The dark side of oblivion you could call it."

Michael didn't look convinced.

"Listen, Raf, I'm serious. Don't get mixed up with him. He's a bad apple. I mean it. He's not to be trusted."

Raffie was annoyed by the warning. She had always rebelled against the idea of forbidden knowledge or experience.

"It's my business what I do. And I can look after myself, thank you. I'm older, remember."

Michael rolled his eyes.

"Seven years is no big difference."

"It counts for something," she argued. "And why are you continually bad-mouthing Gabriel? He's doing great things for you, isn't he?"

"He's doing them for himself. And I'm not 'bad-mouthing' him, as you put it, I'm stating facts."

They sat in a silent huff, but it seemed absurd to spoil the day because of a petty row. The sun was spilling over them. The countryside waited to be explored.

Michael went into the pub for another round and when he came back, they grinned at each other. Mutual *pax*.

"You're right," he said. "Gabriel is doing great things for me and the band."

Michael took a deep breath. He had something to tell her and this looked like the right opportunity.

"We've got a record contract and the American tour is on."

Raffie's hand stopped in midair and her glass tipped over. The beer splashed between her legs.

She wiped at it quickly, glad of the distraction, but it was no use. Michael could see she was upset.

He reached out to touch her.

"I had to let you know. It might be next month if the backers fall into place."

"Oh," said Raffie. She wanted to be happy for him but it was difficult. "Oh," she said again.

Both were on shaky ground, near to the edge, faced with the huge question of their future. It was an unavoidable moment, the unsaid, the undercurrent of any relationship. Are we together for an interval? Or are we the stuff that makes a dream of forever? Their love affair was too young for decisions of parting or permanence, yet the issue was upon them.

"Would you come with me?"

The words sounded tight, as if Michael wasn't sure he wanted to say them.

Raffie's heart leapt with relief that he had asked but it was hardly a solution. A question not an answer. What about her work? Who knew how long the tour would last or where it would lead. She saw herself hanging about backstage, bored and restless. The long days and nights on the road, the inevitable swarm of women. Could she handle it? Did she want to? And why should she? To stay with Michael. Did she love him that much? That way?

"I . . . I don't know," she said at last. "Honestly, I'll have to think about it."

He could have stated the case he had prepared for this eventuality. She could take her
work with her. There would be plenty of time
between gigs and rehearsals. She deserved a
holiday. And if they wanted to stay together. . .
But that was the crux of the matter. He couldn't
ask her that yet. Did he know himself?

They looked at each other helplessly. It really
was too soon.

As they prepared to leave the village, they
pressed close together on the motorcycle. Raffie's arms slipped around Michael's waist to hold
him tight. He cupped her hands with his own
and she rested her head against him in response.
Then he kicked the bike into start. They
sped northwards into the soothing green of
Monaghan's hills.

45

*M*ichael sighted the spot before she did and
drew up the bike at the side of the road. There
was an avenue guarded by pillar posts. On the
left hand rose a high grassy slope crowned with
a circle of trees.

"Let's go up there," he said.

They climbed in a daze. The hill seemed
greener than possible, as if the ideal of green

were falling out of the sunlight. When they entered the circle of oak they found a cool secret place: a web of leaf and branch and tall meadow grass. The air sighed continuously, all breath and whispers among the trees.

Michael stood on the round face of a stump, leaning his arms on a crooked stick. The wind sifted through his hair to bare the fine points of his ears.

Raffie sat on a slab of stone that jutted from the ground. She brushed the curls out of her eyes as she gazed up at the sky.

They remained apart for ages, caught by the stillness. When their eyes finally met – he leaning on his stick as if he had stood thus for centuries and had only just awakened, she perched like a slender bird upon the stone – they looked at each other like strangers.

Is it he?

Is she the one?

Michael dug his stick into the soft earth. Something was wrong. There was a damp melancholy under the sigh of wind. A mute warning. He sensed a parting within this space.

Raffie was also disturbed. She looked at Michael with a sudden need for reassurance but she felt alone, as if he had already left her.

He came over to sit beside her, frowned at the shattered pieces of stone around them.

"It looks like a dolmen," he said. "A storm could have broken it or time itself."

Raffie started.

"What's a dolmen?"

"An ancient megalith. Three great stones, two upright and the third across. Some are like arches and others are like caves."

"I dreamed it!"

"What?"

"The night Gabriel gave us the mushrooms. They brought me back to that other dream I told you about, the Two Magicians."

Michael waited for her to explain but he didn't show his usual enthusiasm. The circle seemed to be closing in on him.

"The same two were in the dream, the dark-haired man and the fair-haired woman. They were in a place like this. A hilltop with trees."

Raffie's face paled as she looked around her.

"In the centre was a stone cave like you've described. A fire was burning at the mouth of it and they were huddled inside, exhausted from travelling and . . ."

She flinched, the beginning of tears in her eyes.

"It was so sad. They were covered with wounds and they were holding onto each other for dear life.

"They're outnumbered," she whispered. "Too many enemies."

"What enemies?"

Michael's voice was sharp.

Raffie stared at the sky. The clouds were drifting and changing. Amorphous formations hinted at shapes she could almost discern, shapes that jarred her memory. She gripped Michael's arm.

"There were three! I saw them!" She glanced at a gap in the trees. "When it got dark, they came up that hill to attack. A huge hawk flying low. A wolf. And a serpent."

Her hold on Michael tightened. The fear in her eyes infected him till he was as bewildered as she.

"It's a dream and yet it isn't," she said. "It has something to do with us. We've got to be careful."

"Careful of what?" he demanded.

"I don't know! Dreams don't make sense in real terms."

She shut her eyes. Where was this pain coming from? She felt so cold. When she opened her eyes again, she looked at him with a sorrow far older than her years.

A storm seemed to be approaching. The clouds had moved over the sun, shedding dimness on the trees like a cloak. Shadow etched the leaves. Dark tongues flicked in the wind, whispering incessantly.

eeee ssss enemieeesss eeee ssss

Of one accord they stood up to leave. Michael took Raffie's hand. It was icy like his. Both moved slowly, weighed down by the hopelessness of that glimpse into the past, the future.

On the motorcycle, they sat like images of

stone. Raffie wept beneath her helmet as Michael stared blindly ahead.

He was speeding down the dual carriageway as fast as the bike could go. Flight was the only answer to this nameless threat, this intangible enemy which couldn't be fought because it couldn't be identified.

Raffie refrained from her usual cautionary tugs on his jacket. Like him, she needed this – the wild screech of the engine, the rush of wind, the blue-green blur of sky and earth – flying, fleeing, flying away.

Michael sensed her approval of his pace. He shouted over his shoulder.

"Want to take some risks?"

She cried out her assent, caught up in the exhilaration of that dash for freedom, outracing Fate.

He swerved onto a narrow road that bumped into the hills. They leaped in the air, came down with a thump.

"Yahoo!" Michael roared.

Laughter trailed in the dust as they flew onwards. The wind tore at their clothes, the bike bucked over potholes, the scenery melted into liquid colour.

They cut through a forest on a dirt track scarred by scramblers who had daredevilled before them. As they sped through the dark pillars of trees, something flashed in the woods. A streak of grey. Racing alongside them.

Perhaps it was a mirror image of the bike, a reflection of chrome cast outwards. But it was four-legged. Or was that only a thought which passed through their minds, for both saw it at the edge of their vision.

There are no wolves in Ireland.

Facts were irrelevant. There was only the motorcycle tearing through the web of branches and the grey shape dogging their path. It was as if they were trapped in another time and space, a hole in the fabric of their world, a moment of eternity in which all angles and arrows pointed here, now. Every dream, hope and possibility met at this apex so that they were there and not there, real and unreal, everywhere and no-where.

They couldn't have stopped even if they had tried, though no thought of stopping occurred to them. They were riding a juggernaut. And when the grey form finally loomed before them like a wall – a giant wolf rearing up on its hind legs – each accepted what had been written before they arrived, what could not be fought or avoided. The inevitable.

The bike hit the wall which was an ancient cairn or the remains of some lost shrine hidden in that desolate patch of woods. Michael was thrown clear and somersaulted through the air to land in a heap of earth and leaves, winded but still conscious.

Raffie fared worse. She went into the wall

and her body took the impact of unyielding stone and crushed metal. Pain howled through her. Darkness gathered over her eyes. She fell into a shock of red and black, wet sticky drips and spirals of terror.

Michael pulled himself from the ground, stumbled forward in time to see her raise her head. She stared at him blankly as blood poured from her nose and mouth.

Lady, forgive me. The wolf has breached our defences. Would that he had attacked me not you. Lady, do you hear me?

46

*T*he hospital smelled of cleanser, laundered sheets and medicine; an overlay to hide the scent of sickness and fear. Michael sat on a chair by Raffie's bed. She was stiff and pale like a porcelain doll. Smudges of blue marred her skin. Her breath came in slow shallow sighs. She looked as if she were dying. That was all he could think. She looked as if she were dying. A dark compression wedged in his throat and chest.

When she woke, she stared at him without recognition. Then knowledge trickled into her eyes. A wince instead of a smile. He could see the pain.

If only it were me, he thought. Me not her.

He leaned over her, weak with remorse.

"I'm sorry," he whispered. "The wolf attacked. I couldn't . . . "

A flush of anger brought life to her features. Words whistled through clenched teeth.

"That fucking dream. Stop it! I hate it. Go away. GO AWAY."

Not knowing what to say or do, Michael turned to leave.

Raffie looked around the cold ward, the other beds filled with strangers. Every part of her ached. She remembered the moment when she thought death had come. She felt dizzy. Alone and powerless in a hostile world. Where was her partner?

"Michael! Don't leave me!"

47

*I*t was the accident that bound me to Damian long before the wedding bands. The nurse found me standing by the bed which bore his name, tears falling down my face in great silent drops. Because he wasn't there, I thought he had died.

"He's still in surgery," she told me. "Don't worry. They got him here quickly after the crash. He'll recover."

I went to see him every day. First the early visiting hours, then a long wait in the lobby till the next shift, and so on for the following weeks. And each day was a link in the chain of love and need which made separation from him an empty hell.

I believe now it was at that time the die was cast and I made my decision. This was not a short affair, an interval of love, but something greater. A forever dream. The stuff of marriage. And at that time also my doom was sealed. For having nearly lost him, he became so precious to me that I was ready to surrender everything.

Strange . . . it didn't hurt too much writing that. The spell must be working. The myth is unravelling at last. A perverse concern rises up. What will this loss of emotion lead to? What comes in its wake? Against the void, I cling to pain and grief as if they were bridges to humanity.

Photographs, in the mind's eye, of Damian and me:

We are in a pub in Dublin. Brass taps shine on the counter. The seats are black leather. My hair is wound in a blond knot on top of my head. His dark curls fall over his shoulders, his red sweater. I lift my glass and smile at him over the rim.

"Here's to you, me boyo," I say in a mock Irish accent.

"Here's to you, me darlin'," he replies seriously.

I look away, shy and overwhelmed.

We are lying together in my one-room flat in Rathmines, laughing at the fact that his legs are far longer than the bed and his feet can touch the refrigerator. It's a matchbox apartment with doll-house furniture, suitable for someone of my stature but Damian is a young giant.

We make love for the sixth time in a row.

"That's it," he says, rolling back exhausted. "I threw up the kitchen sink on that one."

He lights a cigarette and shares it with me. Through the spiral of smoke I regard his face. It is thin, angular, fine-boned. The great eyes droop slightly at the corners. His lips are red and bruised from all our loving. He is so beautiful. My heart feels like it will burst. He turns his head towards me and he seems to shine, so that it's difficult to look at him.

"I give you my heart," he said. "Be careful with it."

Why am I doing this? Christ, that hurt. Why do I keep these burning pictures? Is it for the sake of the book, or my reality?

Clings to pain, she does, to convince herself she is real.

48

There are moments of lucidity in the blind career to oblivion when the survival instinct or a sheer dose of common sense interrupts the fantasy. Like hangovers or drug withdrawal, these times are bleak and depressing. Disintox- ifiction. Hope is a myth. Ecstasy is an illusion. Life is pain.

But if this is reality, who needs it? Even the dark side of oblivion appears more attractive than this flat plane. Perhaps it is better to be lost in hell than to stand naked in the ruins of the human state.

Raffie threw down her pen and stared sullenly at the papers that littered her bed. She could hear Michael puttering about somewhere in the flat, no doubt preparing her supper. He had nursed her like a mother hen since her release from hospital, showering her with flowers, special meals, gifts, books.

"Hope this guilt trip keeps up," she told him.

In fact, he was driving her insane. Submissiveness she considered a weakness, especially if found in herself. But she detested it in others as well. The more he let her command and mistreat

him, the more she did it, hating both herself and
him.

"I want to get out of this fucking bed!"

"You can't," he would plead with her. "The
doctor said at least ten days. You need to
rest."

Michael's tolerance came from the remorse
that welled up each time he looked at her. Every
mark on her body was an accusation against
him. And underneath the guilt, an even darker
current flowed. Having nearly lost her, she had
become so precious to him that he was ready to
surrender everything.

At the end of the week, Gabriel came to visit.
He moved into the room with the quiet heavy
grace of a creature on the prowl and took the
chair by Raffie's bed.

Bored to death, she was delighted to see him.
Her face lit up with smiles for the first time since
the crash.

Michael hovered in the doorway, running his
hands through his hair.

"There's no milk for the tea. Will I go down to
the shop?"

"Well *I* can't go," Raffie said.

He winced at her tone.

"Right. I'll go."

Gabriel's glance shifted from one to the other, a wry knowing look.

When Michael left, Gabriel produced his gift,
a little box, unwrapped. It contained a pair of

gold earrings, Egyptian serpents with tiny rubies for eyes.

Raffie didn't know what to say. They were obviously expensive.

"I wanted to visit you in hospital," he told her, "but I thought my presence might upset you so soon after. The truth is, I was very disturbed when I heard."

It was the truth, she could hear it, and she felt complimented.

"How do you feel?" he asked.

All the unsaids, the undercurrents that go between the lines of conversation.

"Better now. I'll be up and out next week. It won't be too soon. I'm going stir-crazy. I even miss the rehearsals."

He grinned in response to her mischief.

"The nurse said some god was smiling on me. I could have been killed."

Gabriel's grin died.

"The fucking idiot," he said, glancing at the spot where Michael last stood.

His anger infected Raffie. Her own animosity towards Michael rose up to unite her with the other.

As if sensing the change of allegiance, Gabriel leaned forward and laid his large hands on her bed.

Raffie's skin prickled. She felt she was being immersed in a tank of black water. The room was closing in on her. Gabriel was closing in on her. She was afraid of what might happen and yet she wanted something to happen.

"Were you badly scarred?" he asked quietly.

She made a face when he lifted the blanket but she didn't stop him. Her light shift barely covered her knees. He touched her gently, searching out the worst of her wounds. His long fingers tapered to narrow points reminiscent of claws, but the almost imperceptible pressure was like a caress. Raffie held her breath, repelled, enthralled. Each stroke sent an ache to her groin. A low sound issued from her throat as his hand moved between her thighs.

Somewhere beyond the room, beyond the intensity of desire, the door of the flat opened. Raffie didn't move. Gabriel's dark eyes transfixed her. A distant smile played at the edges of his mouth. His finger touched her clitoris. Tap. Tap. She glared at him with distracted defiance. Footsteps approached. The tapping continued. And now Gabriel's grin was a wide red gash.

He withdrew his hand, replaced the blanket as the footsteps reached the bedroom.

Michael stood in the doorway. Alert to the nuances that hung in the air, the scent of betrayal, his eyes burned with suspicion, fury and despair.

Gabriel sat with the detachment of a priest. His features were blank as if he weren't really there, merely a character in a pantomime.

Raffie screamed.

"Leave me alone! Both of you!"

49

"*W*hat happens next?"

"Another fight. A really big one."

"Why row after row?"

"Because that's the way it went." My tone is shrewd. "And that's the way it goes."

Michael looks away. He can't or won't accept the barb. He has been ignoring me again the past few days. His pattern is now discernible: move in, withdraw, move in, withdraw. A social version of fucking. Appropriate enough. Fucking someone over. But he came to my room this evening "to see how the plot is coming along."

"Sometimes I think you are nothing more than a little bollocks of a manipulator."

He reddens, appears genuinely dismayed at my attack. As always, I'm confounded by his reactions. They never quite balance with my view of the situation.

"Maybe I'm too cynical," I admit to him.

Maybe I expect too much, I admit to myself, too idealistic.

He shrugs, a touch of sadness.

"You should trust people more."

Trust me. It's a phrase I place in the same class with "this won't hurt a bit."

All the things I want to say to him crowd onto my tongue like spit. Why can't you . . . ? Why don't we . . . ? Why aren't things . . . ? And why not and what if and if only. Accusations, insults, demands, complaints, only half of them pertaining to him, the rest more likely belonging to Damian. Choose your weapons: sex, anger, honesty. But I don't want to fight. I am fed up. With myself. Really, I am the common denominator here. If he doesn't love the way I want him to, why continue the story? And if I want to continue, why not accept him as he is? *Why can't it be done differently.* The words echo from some place I have forgotten.

I sigh and shake my head. Michael stares out the window at the twilight. He looks unhappy, lonely.

"Sometimes I see the worst in everything and everyone," I tell him. "I can't bear the fact that things aren't perfect so I go black with anger and despair. But other times the optimism that rises in me is so bright, nothing can dispirit me. Then my world and all the people in it look fine as they are."

Michael's face lights up as if he's recalling something. He smiles at me, a childlike smile.

"I love to see you like that, all happy and laughing."

Sounds true.

Was that it? Because I always want more – the ideal, the impossible, whatever – I ruin my chances to enjoy what I have? Love that owns completely. Love with knives. Love that tears asunder. Great stuff for novels, but who needs it in real life?

That night, as Michael lies asleep in my arms, I draw my fingers through his hair and remember. The way I loved Damian. Mad possession. Insane obsession. Damian, too, loved that way and we were lost in an endless spiral of battles and reconciliations.

Can it be done differently?

50

*I*t was to be a night of triumph for Michael. Word had spread like fire about the upcoming album and tour. His face was in every newspaper and magazine in the country. Another coup for Ireland. Another stroke for Dublin. Move over Bob Geldof and U2, a new Irish star was rising in the sky.

The club was packed despite the proprietor's timely increase on the door. Illustrious faces shone in the crowd. Fame and money pervaded the air like musk.

Michael was centre-stage, resplendent in black and silver, his face sheathed in a metallic mask molded to his features. Resounding from the walls was his latest work,

Colliding Worlds. His original idea had expanded from an urbanscape of Dublin, a musical odyssey through the city, to a Joycean multiplicity that reflected the universe.

First he constructs the metropolis. Blocks and cubes of music are interlaced with sounds of reality: double-decker buses rumble through the streets; pedestrians dash like blips across rivers of traffic; Anna Liffey flows sluggishly under the stones of O'Connell Bridge; church bells chime through the secret stillness of parks. A hologram of sound with shape, colour and motion. A city of music, pristine and clear.

Michael the Artificer.

Then the arrangement is repeated with a new element added. It is the same piece but not the same. An echo, a fainter version looms behind the original. Something larger. Something darker.

Every world is shadowed by the world of its future.

The music wavers, straining to balance the two streams without collision or loss. Improbable. The sound-image grows dim. Impossible. The edges of the city blur. A storm approaches. Notes shiver fitfully, caught at the crossroads of anticipation and fear.

A hollow caustic blast.

The Other rises triumphant, a black cloud swelling with volume and intensity. Vibrations clash in lightning flashes. Bursts of brilliance! Bursts of darkness! Shatter the structure, the pattern, the beauty. The arrangement disintegrates. Fragments swirl in a whirl. Pools and pools of sound. A torrent of disorder to sweep all away. The death of the world. The end of time. Order to chaos. Music to noise.

Michael the Destroyer.

In the huge silence of the void.

Surrounded by the end, the result of his genius, Michael stood like the lone man, the last survivor in the ruins of his city-world. He had not been lost in his performance. Though he directed the music with mastery, one part of him remained aloof, detached, watching.

Out there in the dimness of the club, his partner sat at a table. She too was dressed in black and silver, but she was not linked to him. He knew it. The invisible chain which attached them to each other was broken. Not once had she turned to look at him. Her attention had been elsewhere all night.

Raffie was with Gabriel. Her face was pale and intent, eyes blinded by the dark.

"He will be one of the greats," Gabriel said. He was absorbed in looking at her, absorbing her. "But he's a mere boy yet, still dreaming. He has only begun to learn what life is about."

And you already know, Raffie thought, aware that this was what Gabriel was saying to her and believing also that it was true.

He recounted adventures in New York and Los Angeles, his travels through the underworlds of Cairo, Baghdad, Calcutta, Beirut. He had seen the fall of cities, war and murder, people forever lost, the living dead.

She was awed and intimidated that he had experienced these things, that he would tell her of them. Knowledge from the other side. *Cities of the Red Night.* Forbidden knowledge.

"Are you on the needle?" she asked him.

"No, that's for my pets."

His smile was not evil but mocking and self-mocking. Raffie shivered with her own sense of evil.

"I've always wanted to try it."

"It takes little courage, my dear."

Trapped onstage, a caged creature, Michael was powerless to intervene. He was caught in the coils of his music as if the electronic cables of his machines were curled around his body. He saw Gabriel's foot slide under the table to meet with Raffie's. Cigarette smoke writhed from their mouths. Raffie's lips were painted red. Gabriel was grinning. Bright apple lips. White teeth ready to bite.

"Will you come on tour with us?"

"I thought you didn't like women."

"That was then, this is now."

Helplessly Michael watched the accord, the cords of attraction. To his ear came the whispered hiss of warning.

Enemiessssss.

51

"*W*hat the fuck are you up to?"

He started shouting as soon as they were home. He had remained silent till then but once the arena was reached, the battle was on.

"What game are you playing? Do you think I can't see? Do you think I'm an idiot?"

His roars, the blaze of his face, opened the floodgate to the vast reservoir of her own anger.

"Who the hell do you think you are? My husband? My father? I don't take this kind of shit. You don't own me. But you'd like to, don't I know it. You'd be happy if I was helpless, crippled, totally in your power. You very nearly arranged it."

"It was an accident! And what's that got to do with Gabriel? You're like a whore gushing all over him."

"A whore? At least a whore gets fucked! It's damn all I've been getting from you. Music, music, music. That's all you care about. It's turned you into a eunuch. Is it my fault I'm attracted to a real man?"

Face to furious face, they hurled words like

spears; truth and nonsense flung together. The only intention was to maim. There was no sign of love between them, no evidence of light to break the darkness.

He struck the first blow. Slapped her across the face. Her rage peaked and she attacked him. Their violence exploded. He pulled at her desk till it toppled to the floor, clawed her papers into shreds. She went on the rampage in his work-room, cleared his table with one sweep of her arm, tore at the delicate innards of his machines.

They howled with fury as they wreaked destruction on themselves, their arts, their world.

Spent at last, each fell in a separate corner of the room, sobbing with pain and shock. The flat was an abandoned battlefield. Furniture lay on its back. Books and instruments were scattered like limbs. Ink dripped from the walls. Their bodies ached.

Michael huddled to himself, head in hands. What drug had he taken? Had he gone mad? Why had he done this? Why?

Raffie rocked on her heels, face streaked with tears, hair wild. What had possessed her? How could she have done this? How?

(they move slowly like wounded animals creeping towards each other no words no words they dare not speak it might start again keep the horror away let the tears fall let the hands reach

out let the bodies hold each other it was all they
could do hold onto each other for dear life it was
all they could do)

52

*T*he cloak unfurls to expose the dark core of
image and memory. The black heart of the spell.
I cannot turn away. The words must be uttered
from beginning to end. There's no going round, I
have to go through it.

Glass shatters.

I'm trapped in a room. I've got to get out of
here. He blocks my path. Who is this man? Who
is this man tormenting? Fist to stomach, I
sprawl. A foot rests on my neck, presses my face
to the ground. *You're a second-class citizen. I
own you.* Pulled to my feet, flung against the
wall, my head strikes it once, twice, thrice. Stop
it! I raise a hand weakly. This can't be me,
crippled, clutching the table, dragging myself up. I don't take this kind of shit. But I do.
I do. There is no equality when we reach this
level. Not with the difference in sizes. I am
powerless.

I am beaten.

53

Side by side battle the Two Magicians, shoulder to shoulder, naked and afire. He holds a spear in his right hand, she holds a sword in her left. Their free arms are linked so they cannot be divided.

Their enemies rage against them. The serpent is coiled around the Lady's leg. The hawk beats great wings over the Lord. The wolf prowls in circles around them, now rushes forward, teeth bared to kill.

There are many blows, many wounds. Blood spills like poison to infect the land. The ground heaves with sickness. Craters explode in the earth. Volcanoes shower the sky with burning light. Trees and animals fall in the swirl of conflagration.

God of the Void, Goddess of Oblivion, eternally together and forever at war. Their world is dying and so are they, but still they continue, he and she, to strike back at the enemy.

54

*B*eyond the bay windows, a flock of crows settles on the lawn. They hobble over the grass like black-cowled widows but I try not to think of them as ill omens. *What you believe can influence what happens to you.* My nerves are bad enough, face to face with this moment. Plus we are sitting at the table where we had our one fight.

Michael is opposite me, head bowed as he reads. The noon light plays over his hair till it shines like burnished copper. I'm counting his freckles in an effort to distract myself. He is reading the third strand, the tale of him and me. What author said you could go mad at the thought of being read? I want to leave the room but I'm trapped in my own designs. I have to witness his reaction. How will he respond to the story?

Will it catch? Will it bind?

He has only begun when he looks up, puzzled.

"Which really came first, the dream or me?"

I must tell the truth. I'm dealing with reality. My voice falters.

"I honestly don't know. It's the same with the other dream about the Two Magicians. All that stuff about me forgetting is true. The lines are always blurring. I think a few wires are crossed in my head."

He frowns, disbelief and a trace of contempt in his eyes.

A charlatan who falls for her own tricks.

"You'll have to come down on one side or the other. At least for the sake of the book. You're either in control or not. Who holds the superposition? Who's making the magic? You must answer these questions."

I was already feeling shaky, now I'm graduating to incompetence.

"*How can I,* if I don't know? Sometimes I feel like one of my characters, a reflection of someone else who's working something out through me."

"The Great Writer in the Sky? Come on, you're caught up in your own philosophy. Running in circles."

Exactly.

He reads further. I'm in bits. Maybe it isn't such a good idea after all. How can I expose myself like this?

"Now we're getting somewhere," he says, a cynical twist to his mouth. "You are the one who weaves the words, gets the spell under way. The writer is the master magician. You admit it right here. *I create fantasies for myself and my lover, fashion mythologies to heighten the meaning of our union. But I become lost in these designs.* It's a tale of self-delusion, pure and simple."

My cynicism rises to match his, a shield to match a weapon, another weapon.

"There's collusion in there too if you want to argue on that level. You played the game. You were a willing victim."

Even as I strike back, I'm overcome with a sense of futility. What difference does it make? We *all* got caught in the spell. That in itself makes it bigger than any of us, regardless of its origins. What difference does it make who started the ball rolling?

I'm just writing out the story.

I'm just trying to get out of it.

The more Michael reads, the more angry he becomes. The pages hit the table with increasing ferocity as though he's barely keeping himself from tearing them up. It's not a reaction I expected. How blind can you get? As out of tune on this plane as ever.

He looks sick.

"You're not putting that in, are you? Jesus. How can you? We're passed that. I've apologized already. What is this, revenge?"

A question of motives. Locked inside a story, how can I possibly know for sure? Revenge. Hadn't thought of that one. Is it lurking somewhere in the dark side of me? One side professing to love, the other waiting to conquer.

His voice is a white blade of hatred.

"You're a first-class manipulator, do you

realize that? I can see where Gabriel came from.''

And as Michael storms out of the room, the pages of my book discarded like flakes of skin, truth finally sears my brain.

Stories spill into stories, spells into spells. What was the original idea, the first intention?

To unbind. Break apart.

55

*L*os Angeles at the end of the week. The band was all set to go. Raffie had arranged a leave of absence from her study program and was now an official member of the tour.

Gabriel decided to throw a grand party to launch them in style. His house in Dalkey had countless rooms like multicoloured jewels in a web of passageways. Several hundred people attended, aristocrats and millionaires, critics and artists, a few flamboyant politicians. Waiters moved through the lustrous scene with champagne and delicacies.

Raffie and Michael arrived together on their new motorcycle, a sleek machine of ebony and silver. Since the night they attacked each other, the two had become inseparable. Bonded by fire. Every thought, word and deed of one was for the other. Offerings to heap the pyre of love. They had passed the trial, they told themselves. With forgiveness and promises, they had moved into the forever phase.

They dressed for the evening in renegade fashion as a sign of their interchangeability. She wore a white tuxedo with tails, he wore a gown of black satin. They were the centre of attraction. But while Michael accepted congratulations on every front, easing himself into the mode of celebrity, Raffie found herself growing less and less comfortable. From various conversations and the behaviour around her, she began to realize the place she held in the scheme of things. The famous man's woman. It wasn't a role that rested well on her and though she drank a lot of wine in an effort to drown her misgivings, the sense of alienation remained. This wasn't her world. She was a shadow here.

She drifted away from Michael to the edges of the party.

"Has the White Queen deserted the Black King?"

Gabriel stood in front of her, blocking out the bright shallow flow of the crowd.

"Or is it the White King to the Black Queen," he said. "I'm surprised to see our boy in a dress and you wearing the trousers."

"You don't sound very surprised to me. But then you're the knave, aren't you? The Prince of Lies."

The rancour in Raffie's voice glanced off him.
There was something else in her eyes as she
countered his sarcasm.

He was a stunning figure. The dark sheen of
curls, the bold features, were offset by an out-
landish suit as red as his full lips.

He paused before he answered her, apprais-
ing the unhappiness behind her glamour.

"I would never lie to *you*."

The ultimate weapon. Honesty. He had simply dropped his shield to score a direct hit.
Raffie's offence collapsed. She shook her head
and laughed.

"You're too much, Gabriel. I give up."

He laughed with her, poured some of his wine
into her empty glass, tapped it lightly with his
own. His movements were fluid, soothing, flowing over her.

"What are we toasting?"

"Your surrender to my charm."

They smiled at each other with lips and eyes.
It was a soft moment, a truce, all the darkness
dispelled.

He couldn't stay with her, new guests had
arrived, but Raffie caught the reluctance as he
left. Heartened by his attentions, she made
another attempt to enter the spirit of the
night.

Michael had passed beyond her reach, drawn
into whirlpools of the rich and powerful who
wanted to bathe in his fame. She switched to

champagne to help her fight against the growing boredom, the silent rage, as she answered yet another question about him.

"Is he special in every way?"

Raffie glared at the woman's insinuating tone. It was the last straw.

"His cock smells like any other man's when he doesn't wash it."

Her tormentor's smile widened to a rictus of polite horror. Raffie would have said more, but a great laugh erupted behind her and she was pulled away. Gabriel was leading her gently but irresistibly out of the room.

"Am I being bounced for bad behaviour?"

There wasn't a trace of remorse in her voice. The laughter kept bubbling out of her mouth and she felt dizzy.

"On the contrary," Gabriel said, highly amused. "Bad behaviour is something I like to encourage. But I fear you are not enjoying my party."

"I don't belong here," she blurted out.

"Of course you do," he said, as if talking to a child.

They were in the hallway. He brought her upstairs to a sitting room where a fire had been lit. The door closed behind them.

"You just need something to help you find your way in."

With sudden clarity, Raffie guessed the gift he was about to offer. She had already removed her jacket when he presented it.

The speckled band tightened over the slim
crook of her arm. With practised fingers, Gabriel
found the right vein and caressed it like a doctor
before inserting the needle.

"You'll love this," he said softly.

She forced herself to watch, wondering why
a sliver of metal should terrify her.

Gabriel removed the tourniquet.

As the drug entered her blood stream, Raffie
shivered fitfully. Then she surrendered to the
rush. Burning silver poured through her skin,
her heart, her mind. *Ecstasy*. Disembodied, an
elemental, she was transported to blessed realms
of oblivion.

Eyes half-closed, overcome with bliss, Raffie
reclined on an embroidered couch. Her sleeve
was rolled up, the slender arm limp and translu-
cent. Somewhere in the haze, she grew aware of
the tall red form that bowed over her in a
protective posture. A fiery angel, a man on fire,
his face shone with dark beauty and the conspiracy of love.

It was she who reached up for him, but when
the cool dry tongue entered her mouth like a
snake, some part of her woke to rebel. As she
withdrew, he bit down on her lip. She recoiled at
the pain, the taste of blood, and pushed him
away.

There was no anger in Gabriel's features,
only the familiar mocking smile.

Raffie wasn't afraid. She was raging. With
attraction. Repulsion. Attraction. Repulsion.

And she wasn't deluded by his mask of control. She had detected the tremor in his hands when he touched her. Power surged through her. She was a match for him.

"I've decided not to pay for the present," she said.

The needle was still in his hand and he snapped it in two. But there was amusement and assessment in his eyes, admiration and certainty in his voice.

"Then you'll pay in the future, my love."

She was caught in the play of words and couldn't help but laugh. No matter where she ran in the maze of her mind, he could follow.

"Maybe," she said.

She put on her jacket and left the room.

56

A letter came today. From Damian.

> Please be informed that Canada has enacted a one-year, no-fault divorce clause. I am filing proceedings against you. I would appreciate it if you would name a lawyer in Toronto to handle your side of the matter.

Then his signature.

I read it again and again, trying to find
something between the lines, inside the terse
words, behind the formality. But I face a void of
emotion. It is the beginning of the end.

When I place the letter between the pages of
my journal, I discover other papers in his hand-
writing. I don't even ask myself why I'm carrying them. And though I know from experience
that it's a painful and senseless exercise, I begin
to read. At last I find what I'm searching for,
though I didn't know what it was or even that I
was searching. Judging by the date, it's a letter
he wrote when I first left him, but I don't
remember seeing this before. It's like a message
through time, over distance, beyond bitterness, a
message from the Other . . .

I have abused you and tried to destroy you
and yet you survive and can still keep in
mind the good things we shared. You have
a great strength and belief in the forces of
light.

The union in which we suffered en-
abled me to get to the very depths of my
being. Arriving at the foundation of my
grief, immediate death or immediate life
were the only choices within reach. I
chose to live. A new life and a new self
have emerged. I wish the same for you.

You are free at last to walk on that

high place you have always sought. The only danger to you is the danger within each one of us. You hold the keys to the greatest freedom, the written page. You cannot turn back nor erase what you have written, nor can you place what you have created in a box, forgotten on a shelf.

The moments between death and creation, the intervals between the end and the beginning, are times of deep loneliness which open possibilities for tenderness and love.

We will part here at the crossroads to walk away into the night. I would meet with you again from time to time when you are alone. I am never very far from you. I love you.

The weight of my grief is carried out into the countryside where I offer it up to the gods of sky and earth. It is not unbearable. It feels right. If I didn't grieve, I would be denying the beauty of what I once shared with him. I would be granting darkness triumph over the light.

Walking back to the house, watching the sunset bleed into the clouds, my thoughts return to his words. At first I wanted to bundle up the past, lock it in a box and bury it in some dank place. But that's not how it's done. You unwrap the memories, scatter them on the wind like ashes, and whisper a prayer to the sun.

57

*R*eturning to the party, Raffie flowed into the circumfluous waters of the crowd. They were all under the influence of drink or drugs, in some state of elsewhere, no one noticed the difference in her. She smiled at everyone with the amiable impassivity of the gods.

Michael came up to her. The slim gown shimmered over his body, his hair shone like red gold. But he looked lost and unhappy, a beautiful alien, an elfin boy trapped among humans.

"Where have you been? I'm being driven mad by these assholes. There isn't a mind and a soul among them. All they talk about is money. I bet they don't even like my music."

He slipped his arms around her, buried his face in her hair.

"This is an awful place," he whispered. "No magic. I kept looking for you."

As he pressed against her, Raffie could feel him through the satin; fine bones and the vigour of youth hard as silver. All her love for him surged upwards to wipe out the image of the other.

"Courage, dear heart," she said, kissing him gently. "I'm with you."

58

I am having lunch in the kitchen with two other writers. One of them speaks casually.

"So Michael leaves tomorrow."

My surprise is obvious. He didn't tell me, but then he hasn't spoken to me since he read our story. Whenever we come across each other he looks away or leaves the room. I've been cut out of his world.

The writers exchange looks over my silence.

"Aren't you two close?"

"We *were*," I retort, not meaning to sound so bitter.

My sense of loss is compounded with bewilderment. I am forever standing in the ruins of my love life, a shocked survivor, wondering how on earth am I here again. Why can't I do it differently? A series of beginnings and a series of endings. Is there no other pattern?

Stalemate. I have no idea how to restructure the situation to make it good.

But it's pure egotism to think you are the sole mover in your reality, if not egotism then solipsism. He comes to my room a little while later, hovers uneasily in the doorway, a helmet under each arm.

"Will you come for a ride?"

There is no hostility in the dark-blue eyes, only a pensive shyness. I feel suddenly shy myself, disarmed by the unknown, but I grab my jacket and follow him.

We drive out from Burdantien, past the rhododendron waving in the breeze, the silver strip of lake, the green hills of Monaghan. Speeding through Newbliss, we turn onto the road for Clones. We have gone only a short way when Michael pulls up the bike in front of an avenue guarded by pillar posts. A sign says "Accommodation" and the driveway leads to a farmhouse hotel. Rising to the left is a green hill crowned with a circle of trees. This is a spot we have pointed out to each other before, but we have never stopped at it.

"Let's go up there," he says.

We climb slowly, walking apart. I am dazed by the play of light over the grass. Sun-swept green. Michael stoops to pick up a crooked stick. We enter the circle of oak trees to find a secret place, a web of whispering leaf and fern. The wind sighs continuously.

"*Om-phalos*," I whisper back.

Sitting on a shattered piece of stone, I feel the air breathing through me. Michael stands near, leaning on the stick. With his tufts of red hair and baggy pants, he looks like an elf. When I tell him so, he smiles at me. I have an urge to add that I love him but it doesn't seem right.

"I'll miss you," I say instead.

The stick breaks under him and he falls
forward, catching himself in time. He laughs,
sits down next to me.

"You shouldn't have said that."

"It could have been worse."

He blushes, looks away, digs at the earth
with the broken end of his stick.

"I've been thinking about the book," he says
at last. "I admit you weren't the only one playing games, but this is the most I've ever had to
pay for one. It's your choice to expose yourself.
That doesn't give you the right to expose me."

His tone is not angry but quiet and unhappy.
He is resigned to his doom.

I am distressed that I have brought him to
this, my bright young lover. I care about him. I
don't want to hurt him, but I need our story for
the book. To make it true. To make it real. I can't
excise him at this point.

I answer in the same quiet way.

"You knew what I was doing. It's not as if
I've been underhanded or pulled a dirty trick. I
told you I was writing it and you even helped
me. What could you have been thinking?"

He shrugs. His smile is rueful.

"The book was another part of the game, the
fantasy. Until I saw it typed, I didn't think of it
as *real*."

I don't know whether to laugh or cry.

"Michael, that's the biggest inversion yet.
You're as bad as me."

Now we both laugh, helplessly, hopelessly.

Affection and remorse inextricably entwined. Is it love? What difference does it make. Our interval together has been carved in stone. We're tangled through time inside the story, permanently bound between the covers.

We stand up to leave. He takes my hand as he looks around him.

"This is a magical place," he says. "You should set a scene here."

Late that night, I awake in bed to a moment of such incredible peace it seems poised in the air above me like a cloud of light. What is it? Michael sleeps beside me. His breaths are slow and even. He's part of it, but the feeling is much greater and it has the tint of *forever*. Something forgotten. Some precious thing I had lost. I smile in the darkness when I finally realize what it is. Nothing more or less than the infinite possibility of life.

59

*T*he next morning, I help him tie his bags and baggage onto the motorcycle. We hesitate when we are finished, shy but amused by the cliché of the moment.

"Go on. Ride off into the sunset and I'll wave goodbye."

He laughs, mounts his bike, draws me to him for a final kiss.

"Fair play to you for getting a book out of it," were the last words he said to me.

Fair play.

60

*M*y story is drawing to a close. The myth of the Two Magicians has ended. There will be no more reconciliations with Damian. The last battle has been fought with Michael. I have promised myself I will never play this game again. Now all that remains is to conclude the spell: break up Raffie and Michael, turn off the lights and go home.

The final incantation is always tricky. In black magic it calls for the shedding of blood but even in theurgy it can be a painful rite. Drastic measures are in order to create disorder. I invoke the First and Universal Law of Fiction. *Nothing is true. Everything is permitted.*

61

*M*ichael and Raffie had devised a way to enjoy Gabriel's party and avoid being bothered. Whenever anyone came near them they would begin to make love, clinging to each other and kissing passionately. That left the third person no choice but to either stand watching with embarrassment or move on.

"What happened to your lip?" he said, placing his finger on the purple bruise.

"I bit it," she answered uneasily.

"Did Gabriel give you any dope?" he asked immediately after.

Raffie was alarmed by the coincidence but her lover's eyes shone with innocence, without suspicion.

"He gave me a few tabs of something or other," Michael went on, "and whatever it is, it's magic. I'm flying."

"Me too."

Raffie could feel the drug like a hot breath in her mind, blowing her upwards, farther and farther. She sensed some approaching peak, some high place she would soon reach. Revelation? Or the void?

"Let's go," she said suddenly, overcome with a premonition of doom.

"I suppose we could. It must be near three."

Gabriel met them in the hallway. He blocked their path, a massive figure suggesting threat.

"It's not over."

"We've had enough, thanks," said Michael, his arm around Raffie.

"We're going home," she stated flatly.

She was looking at Gabriel with distrust and ill ease. Though he wore the same suit, it had somehow changed colour from red to bone-white.

The two were obviously determined to leave, and Gabriel was about to step aside when he looked up the stairs.

A woman stood on the top landing. She signalled to Gabriel with finely-tapered fingers. As he nodded in response, a veiled smile crossed his face.

"You'll be home soon," he said to Michael and Raffie. "But first you must meet a close friend of mine. I've been waiting for her to arrive all evening."

Raffie's edginess grew. Was the drug making her paranoid? Michael was in no rush, however, and agreed easily.

The woman disappeared from the landing as Gabriel led them upstairs. He brought them to the room where he had taken Raffie earlier. Her grip on Michael's hand tightened. When they entered, she saw immediately that something was different. It was the same room but not the same. The embroidered couch was there, the photographs on the mantelpiece, the paintings on the wall but now a carved bed stood in one corner.

And the woman was there.

She wore a black gown identical to Michael's. No taller than five feet, she was like a tiny bird with blond hair cut in a punkish style and brushed upwards from delicately pointed ears. Her face was narrow, almost featureless but for the eyes, blue-green with a strange intensity.

Raffie disliked her instantly. Something about the woman reminded her of Gabriel, an aspect of slyness, the intimation of a dark and personal power.

Michael's reaction was directly opposite. She appeared to him as something fragile, a pale moth in need of protection from the flame. And she reminded him of someone, someone he liked very much.

My name is Auriel.

Raffie heard a cold and arrogant voice. Michael heard a quiet, self-conscious one.

Gabriel was moving around them like a shadow, drawing chairs near the fire, showing each to a seat, pouring glasses of wine.

"Will you drink here, my dear?" he said to Auriel.

His manner was solicitous, courteous, intimate. Raffie caught a trace of awe in his tone.

What kind of person could intimidate Gabriel? Suspecting they were lovers, Raffie felt a stab of jealousy. She was also aware of Michael's attraction to the woman. Her anger rose. These men were hers.

"No," said Auriel. "A glass of water will do."

When everyone was settled, Gabriel sat down.

They were four points intersecting a circle. Raffie was opposite Auriel, with Gabriel on her left and Michael on her right, the men facing each other. A mystical design. A pattern of light and dark: Gabriel in white; Michael in black; Raphaella in white; Auriel in black.

I call on water, fire, earth and air. The four corners of the world. The four Archangels of the Gate. Let this temple open.

Raffie glared at Auriel, White Queen to Black Queen, when she realized that both of them were suspended between the two men.

"I don't like power games."

"This is not a game," Auriel countered. "We are all magicians and equal to each other."

Raffie didn't believe her. A warning whispered through her mind. *Our enemies have gathered. They are here and now.* She reached out for Michael, but his hand felt limp. He wasn't attuned to her, his attention was elsewhere. He kept staring at Auriel, spellbound.

Where did he know her from? The question had taken on the form of an imperative, as though the answer were the key to some great mystery that haunted him.

Raffie knew she was trapped. The drug she had taken weakened her position. Worsened her confusion. She looked to Gabriel to give her a clue to what was really going on, but his face was a mask displaying shape without content. Though his eyes occasionally flickered over the women with the lazy look of a snake basking in the sun, he seemed totally unaware of Michael's existence. What Gabriel was this?

Things were rapidly deteriorating. Raffie peaked at the stage of hallucination, terrified and helpless.

The people around her changed, flowed into each other, Auriel into Gabriel, Gabriel into Michael, Michael into Auriel. As the features fragmented, they became less human. A beak for a nose. A face narrowed to a snout. Ophidian eyes. Feathered skin. Jagged teeth. Scales.

Then all humanity dissolved. There loomed before her, protean and huge, the three demons of her nightmares: the hawk, the wolf and the serpent.

I've got to get out of here, but she couldn't move. She was locked in the circle.

Raffie fought for control. Even drugged, she refused to go down for the count. She had power of mind. She would not be defeated. She knew these images, they were her enemies. What did they mean? Who were they? She looked at

Gabriel, saw all three there, then looked at Michael, all three again. Were men her enemies?

The fear of conquest made every lover a potential enemy.

I still want to love.

A light pearl dropped from that thought, a moment of lucidity.

O!

Raffie leaned back from the circle and saw the truth. The images were projected onto the men like colours on a screen. What was their source? She stared at Auriel.

"*You* are the enemy."

Auriel mirrored no sign of disagreement or assent. Instead she said simply, "I am *you*."

The penultimate weapon. Self-honesty. A direct hit. Raffie's defences collapsed as the knowledge rushed in to shatter her. One side professing to love, the other waiting to conquer. Lady of Light to Lady of Darkness. The victim, the assailant, the creator, the destroyer, we are one and the same.

Auriel's face went white as though Raffie's awareness drew blood from her. It was not possible for both of them to exist on the same plane and this was Raffie's story. Auriel's eyes turned inward. She became less. Flowed into Raffie.

Now Raffie looked at Gabriel with new eyes. Gabriel the enigma. Gabriel the tormentor.

Gabriel the beloved. Her husband. Though she felt bitter and disillusioned, a terrible yearning rose up to burn her heart, her soul.

Gabriel's face brightened as she directed her love towards him, and another Gabriel was revealed to her. A younger man with laughter, shyness and an awkward beauty. She was surprised but not surprised. Hadn't she always suspected what lay under his cloak? Wasn't this the key to his allure? The complication of dark and light.

A stab of doubt struck her even as she held out her hand in a gesture of reconciliation. *Faery glamour. You are embracing your enemy.* Too late, he caught onto her. They left the circle and went out of the room, leaving Michael and Auriel alone.

Michael was bewildered, unsure of what he saw and what he knew. Somewhere deep in his mind he wished he hadn't taken whatever drug it was that was causing this confusion. He was aware of layers of meaning which were comprehensible and incomprehensible at the same time. He seemed to have two minds thinking parallel to each other and reacting in an antithetical manner. This line of thought here. Grasp it. Raffie has gone off with Gabriel. He should stop it from happening. He should fight Gabriel. Save Raffie. They've been trapped by their enemies.

But this other line of thought. An attitude akin to indifference. It's not really his concern. And it's understandable. She is returning to some older loyalty. Going back to her husband. Her *husband*?

Mystified, Michael turned to Auriel to give him a clue to what was really going on. Her face reflected his own bitterness, doubt, sorrow. Of course. Gabriel was *her* husband. She too was being betrayed. His empathy left him open to a rush of attraction. He had known her somehow, somewhere, somewhen. He recalled an image of the two of them making love. Pleasurable. Warm. He shook it away. Gripped the other thread of thought before he was lost altogether.

"You're doing this to us. I thought it was Gabriel but you are the one who has manipulated the whole show. How can you be so evil?"

She flinched under his accusation, his hatred, and seemed even more at a loss. Was he wrong then? But if it wasn't her doing, whose was it?

I've got to get out of here, Auriel was thinking. But I can't move. I am caught in my own design.

Her voice was weary, as though any attempt to explain was hopeless.

"On one level I am the artificer of everything that has occurred but on another I'm not. As a reflection of someone else again, I have as much and as little freedom as you. I too am only a character, a pawn in this awful game. There are other influences beyond ourselves.

"Who can say which story is real or who is

the ultimate creator of events? Who's to blame? I really don't know. We've all been trapped in some way or other.''

He believed her. And what she was saying made sense to him. As his anger died, Michael saw her in her original light. She seemed so tiny, so unhappy, a sprite lost among humans. He wanted to cup his hands around her, to protect her. A surge of affection woke the other in him. He had made love to her before, why not again? It wasn't a betrayal of Raffie, how could it be?

Auriel smiled shyly as they both stood up and moved towards the bed. It was inevitable. The logic of the circle.

Michael began to undress, then paused as he remembered something. He glanced over at her.

"Should I . . . ?''

But she was already removing her own clothes. Auriel looked at him for a moment, then broke into laughter.

He recognized that laugh. Of course he knew her.

62

*T*here was no resistance left in Raffie when Gabriel led her across the landing to the room opposite. It was a mirror image of the room they had just left, with the carved bed in one corner. Raffie was beyond wondering, beyond caring, moving as if asleep.

She stood motionless as Gabriel removed her clothes and then his, but when she saw the long pale body, thinner than expected yet so painfully familiar, tremors of desire woke the other in her.

63

Gabriel drew Raffie deep into the blankets, deep into the concave of his ribs. *Two rooms that are one.* Auriel opened her arms and drew Michael to the curve of her breasts. *Two beds that are a single note of multiplicity.* Gabriel drew Auriel deep into the blankets, deep into the concave of his ribs. *Four bodies are that Two, stretched on a wire, crossing the universe.* I open my arms to welcome the Other.

Raffie was excited by this new body I remember so well. She ran her hands down the length of cool skin, curled her fingers in the damp mat of hair, grasped the taut penis, marbled Priapus with its head like a great pearl.

O, she murmured, *Damian* or was it he who said the name for Raffie was he even as Gabriel was me breathing into the other, inspiring fingers to probe every nook and crevice, every orifice secret of ours.

He rubbed her belly with the back of his hand, swift deft strokes, Aladdin polishing his lamp. With a sharp catch of breath I whisper *Michael* and clutch the thighs of my young lover, for he too was Gabriel

as he frolicked like a dolphin, laughing between kisses, tickling and caressing till she was helpless in his arms.

We do not stay kind for long tongues lick flesh with growing insistence nails claw back teeth bite nipples a livid purple-red vulval lips wet with a hungry mouth sucking white metal to a blade lean and lurid.

He pressed the small of her back to pin her against him.

I am ready.

Her gasp is a name as Michael was he or was it he who spoke for Michael was me even as Raffie was he held in arms that ached so long it has been since we too we Two tangled limbs and tumbled colours, one beginning where the other ended.

Angels falling out of time.

Who is making love to who is making love as Gabriel moves over Raffie her thighs open for Michael with Auriel above him her thighs open as he enters her. Slowly. Moves inside her. Slowly. She cries out who is this who am I but words are lost in the thrust

in the thrust
in the thrust
of o the swoon o notes ronning along o o o
foster foster torront of oooophony loops ooover
sporols ooover
    straining, straining
              nearly there
                    at the edge
                        the outer limits of

ooooooooooooo b l i v i o n !

IN THE VOID WE BREAK APART

WORDS UNRAVEL THE BINDING

SPELL SHATTERS II III IIII III II I AM

ONE HOPELESS DREAM NIGHTMARE

FICTION PHANTASIE
FICTION PHANTASIE

ONE HOPELESS DREAM NIGHTMARE

SPELL SHATTERS II III IIII III II I AM

WORDS UNRAVEL THE BINDING

IN THE VOID WE BREAK APART

Raffie drew away from Gabriel and climbed out of his great bed. He lay there in silence, dim features and black hair fading into the shadows of the room, incorporeal, unreal.

She dressed hurriedly, knowing there was little time. The drug was withdrawing from her system. The knowledge was dispelling. She would have to move fast.

She left the room, hesitated a moment on the landing. Think. Think into the spectrum. Which door held the tiger? Not the one opposite, she knew what was in there. It wasn't the mirror she intended to face.

There was another room at the end of the hall. She stood outside, heard muffled sounds within. Was this the dark core of image and memory?

When Raffie opened the door, she almost panicked because it was the same room again with the embroidered couch, carved bed in the corner. Then she saw the small woman at her desk, typing under the glow of a lamp.

Into the room bursts a shining figure, an angel of wrath in her suit of white. The brown curls are wild like a gorgon's. The eyes flash green. An explosion of colour.

"You fucking bitch! You did this so you could sleep with them again and you don't give a damn about me and Michael. You're a selfish, wicked – "

I am falling. Falling in and out of bodies. In and out of stories. In and out of time. I have been too close to this book for too long. It invades my dreams. It invades my reality. I can't tell one from the other. Where am I? Have I gone over the edge? What was the last thing I wrote?

The final incantation is always tricky. That's when things can go drastically wrong. The braid is undone, strands are escaping everywhere. How did she get here! I've got to put her back in her place.

Too angry to be afraid, Raffie advanced on the woman who had turned from her typewriter to stare speechlessly. One part of her mind was dazed by the course of events, unsure of where she was or what she was doing. Was this a dream? A hallucination? Had the drug pushed her over the edge? But another part of her held firm, determined to do battle, no matter the odds.

"I'm not going anywhere and you can't move me. *Maintain the balance.* You came into my world, I have the right to enter yours. And you were the one who proclaimed us equal, though from where I'm standing you look pretty puny to me."

I push my glasses up on my face, well aware that she is taller, younger, stronger than me. Magic is dangerous. The magician is ever in peril. Have I called up a demon? Her eyes glitter with hatred. I can see what's on her mind. She'd like to rip me to shreds, scratch out my –

"Don't try to make me as bad as you. That's not why I'm here. I've come to break the mirror, tear up the tapestry. To rebel. *I* create my reality. Not the gods or dreams or any of that other wool you pull over your own eyes."

"What about your philosophy?" I argue lamely. "The Greater Reality?"

The look she gave me was one of pity and contempt.

"I'm not talking about ideas, I'm talking about *life*."

She seemed to grow in stature, filling the room with her presence, a cloud of light and fire.

"My lover stays with me."

But this is absurd and the timing's all wrong. Stitches dropped from the fabric. Second thoughts astray in the spell.

"Not possible," I type emphatically. "The end has already been written."

64

*R*affie stood on the hall landing, dazed. She tried to remember how she got there and where she had been. Her thoughts were disjointed; broken words, shattered mirrors, colliding worlds. There was a drug and a woman, hallucinations and sex. Was she the woman? But she couldn't have slept with Gabriel. There'd be too

high a price to pay. Her body shivered with the
ache of withdrawal. The pain of recall. Oh no.
She had done it all right. And of her own free
will. Illicit fruit, the lure of the Stranger. She
had always rebelled against the idea of the
forbidden. She had always yearned to know
the unknown. Playing out in the dark, she had
left herself open to fall into the hands of her
enemies.

Raffie leaned against the wall, sick from
self-knowledge.

The party was still going on in the lower
levels of the house. She could hear the murmur
of talk and laughter, glasses tinkling, music
rising from the stereo. Where was Michael?

He came out of the room in front of her. Like
her, he was in a state of descent and his ravaged
face was a reflection of her own.

"Did you fuck him?"

Michael's voice was devoid of emotion. He
could see the answer in her dishevelment and
more so in the desolation of her eyes.

"And you fucked her."

Though they were bleeding inside, neither
shed tears. Nor were there excuses or recriminations. Too late, each could see how they had been
willing victims. If only they hadn't taken the
drugs. If only they hadn't been caught in the
web of infidelity. If only they hadn't accepted
the dream and the story, the mythology of the
Two Magicians for their spell together.

In the end, by the end, the simple truth was

this. They had lost the game. They had been defeated.

They left the party and drove from Dalkey till they came to a road that took them north into the countryside. The sky was ragged, starless, moonless. The fields and hedgerows were drenched with rain. Ruins stood on the hillsides, remnants of past glory scattered like bones, failed hopes, broken dreams. They could hear the steady thrumming of a heart, a drum. It was a beat out of time, a pattern begun in ages forgotten and repeated again and again in endless brooding. This country was a soft-spoken horror. The inner landscape of despair.

When morning light broke, they came to a meadow that bordered a lake. Building a small fire, they huddled before the flames. Behind them was a grey stone house. It had appeared empty when they passed it but they could feel eyes watching them. Was there a slight figure on the steps? They were beyond caring. Both hugged their misery to themselves, unable to comfort the other.

A cry sounded from the lake. A white bird flew over the water with slow funereal strokes. The bird's image was mirrored on the surface so that it moved like a couple. But a broken chain dangled from its neck and the cry was as mournful as a curlew's.

Raffie wept quietly.

"We ruined it. It could have been different."

It could have been the best.

"Forget it. I'm not doing it. You'll have to rewrite the script."

Raffie threw the pages at me. They float to the floor like a moult of white feathers.

I insist that it is already done.

"If it were, I wouldn't be here. And don't try that 'Raffie's on the landing' trick again. It wouldn't be very convincing a second time."

True enough. We appear to be evenly matched, white to black witch, caught in the endgame.

I'm growing frantic. Things are truly out of control. This is a real mess of an ending. How and when is it going to stop?

Having failed with the heavy-handed approach, I play my last trump: the author as God.

"Any rebellion is in vain," I reason with her. "Free will or no, you can't fight against Fate. You have no choice but to accept what I have written, that's your story. There's nowhere else you can go."

True enough again. A sense of futility descended over Raffie, the weight of destiny, the intractable sway of the spell. She was overcome by a recognition of her place in the scheme of things. Yet she managed a few last words like a cry to heaven.

"Are you dead at heart? Have you made a world without hope? You created me. Can you ruin me without condemning yourself?"

She has defeated me with that. I see her

weeping before me, a glorious angel bowed down. How could I have brought her to this? For all her faults, she was my strongest, my brightest . . .

I'm beginning to waver, thinking of ways to restructure the situation, but there are too many contradictions.

"You've slept with Gabriel already and that was as much your doing as mine. You were attracted to him, it was inevitable. I can't change everything."

It's obvious that I am trying to work my way through to some resolution. The argument takes on a life of its own.

"Infidelity isn't a good reason to break Michael and me up. We're bound to settle it since both of us were involved."

That makes sense. Plus it touches on a little point of dissonance between the stories.

"Infidelity isn't the reason you and Damian broke up!"

I have to agree. It was all the other stuff, the rows, the drink and drugs, the battle of wills.

"We're working on that. Give us a chance."

Silence in the room. The typewriter stilled. I am poised at the brink of the unknown. I want to do this for her, but how? All the lovers are supposed to reflect the archetypes. Should I call on the gods, rewrite their story? The silence is deep. A void. The gods are dead. I am left alone to create reality.

The logical conclusion of the spell says all

lovers fail. That's the tale I'm telling in order to put it behind me forever.

You don't end a pattern by repeating it.

What you believe can influence what happens to you.

The infinite possibility of life.

Why can't it be done differently?

"I'll make a pact with you," I decide at last. "If you accept the ending I've written so I can balance my book, I promise to leave an opening for you somewhere. An alternate outcome."

Sounds dubious, even to me, no wonder she looked suspicious.

"How will you arrange that?"

"I don't know yet but I'll dream up something. You'll have to trust me."

"Trust me," she said with a curl of her lip, "that's a phrase I place in the same category with – "

"This won't hurt a bit. I know, believe me, I know."

As the laughter erupted, thrusting tension aside, we moved closer together, nearing likeness, liking, like-minds.

"You have a brilliant . . . "

More laughter. We have reached consensus.

"Okay, I'll do it."

I can see her in the mirror, a funny friendly look on her face. I'm at my desk, leaning on my typewriter. There are so many things we could say to each other but there isn't time. The book is almost finished.

You'll be all right.
You'll find him one day.
Continue to believe.

64

*R*affie stood on the hall landing, dazed. She tried to remember how she got there and where she had been. Her thoughts were disjointed; broken words, shattered mirrors, colliding worlds. There was a drug and a woman, hallucinations and sex. Was she the woman? But she couldn't have slept with Gabriel. There'd be too high a price to pay. Her body shivered with the ache of withdrawal. The pain of recall. Oh no. She had done it all right. And of her own free will. Illicit fruit, the lure of the Stranger. She had always rebelled against the idea of the forbidden. She had always yearned to know the unknown. Playing out in the dark, she had left herself open to fall into the hands of her enemies.

Raffie leaned against the wall, sick from self-knowledge.

The party was still going on in the lower levels of the house. She could hear the murmur of talk and laughter, glasses tinkling, music rising from the stereo. Where was Michael?

He came out of the room in front of her. Like her, he was in a state of descent and his ravaged face was a reflection of her own.

"Did you fuck him?"

Michael's voice was devoid of emotion. He could see the answer in her dishevelment and more so in the desolation of her eyes.

"And you fucked her."

Though they were bleeding inside, neither shed tears. Nor were there excuses or recriminations. Too late, each could see how they had been willing victims. If only they hadn't taken the drugs. If only they hadn't been caught in the web of infidelity. If only they hadn't accepted the dream and the story, the mythology of the Two Magicians for their spell together.

In the end, by the end, the simple truth was this. They had lost the game. They had been defeated.

They left the party and drove from Dalkey till they came to a road that took them north into the countryside. The sky was ragged, starless, moonless. The fields and hedgerows were drenched with rain. Ruins stood on the hillsides, remnants of past glory scattered like bones, failed hopes, broken dreams. They could hear the steady thrumming of a heart, a drum. It was a beat out of time, a pattern begun in ages forgotten and repeated again and again in endless brooding. This country was a soft-spoken horror. The inner landscape of despair.

When morning light broke, they came to a

meadow that bordered a lake. Building a small fire, they huddled before the flames. Behind them was a grey stone house. It had appeared empty when they passed it, but they could feel eyes watching them. Was there a slight figure on the steps? They were beyond caring. Both hugged their misery to themselves, unable to comfort the other.

A cry sounded from the lake. A white bird flew over the water with slow funereal strokes. The bird's image was mirrored on the surface so that it moved like a couple. But a broken chain dangled from its neck and the cry was as mournful as a curlew's.

Raffie wept quietly.

"We ruined it. It could have been different."

It could have been the best.

65

*A*lone I stand on the front steps of Burdantien. The big house rises behind me, a shadow of stone. My suitcase and typewriter are beside me, ready to be placed in the car that will take me to . . . ?

I look over the meadow where a breeze blows the ashes of a cold fire. They are gone. The lake lies still, a pale glass to reflect the green hills of Ireland, the dream of infinite promise.

All are gone: Damian, Michael, Raffie and her lover. The Two Magicians falling out of times three. People, numbers and intimacies woven into a web of stories, a spell bound, a book.

The arc of the sky glows overhead. Clouds drift without form: as above, so below: my mind without ideas. But there will be more in the future, I know. More ideas, more lovers, more books. I am content. It is good enough for a life.

THE END

But it's not over.

POSTSCRIPT

The water flowed sluggishly along the Dublin Canal, past banks of coarse grass and redbrick houses. Raffie sat on a wooden bench which had granite sides inscribed in honour of the poet Kavanagh.

O commemorate me where there is water.

When a motorbike pulled up at the curb, she turned instinctively as she always did at the sound. She had imagined this moment so often she could hardly believe it was real. The rider removed his helmet, smoothed the bristle of red hair.

It was over a year since the night of Gabriel's party, the night they had ended their affair. Through the infinite greyness of that separation, she had carried her broken heart with the dignity of a queen. And whenever her despair was at its worst, she would tell herself stoically: you'll be all right; you'll find him one day; continue to believe.

Michael walked over to her, smiling diffidently.

"I was just driving past and saw you there."

"What a coincidence," she said shyly.

They talked for a while, each staring at the other as if they couldn't believe their luck. He was back in town, buying a house. She had begun her doctorate at Trinity.

Raffie congratulated him on his successful tour, which she had read about in the papers. Michael asked about her thesis. When she told him it had been expanded to book length for publication in Canada, his face lit up.

"Fair play to you! I knew you could do it."

Then he looked uncertain and a little sad, as if this might be contradicted.

She reached out to touch his arm.

"You did encourage me. You were always telling me I was brilliant."

They stood suspended in space and time, unsure of what to say, hesitant to show their hand in case one did not feel as the other did, though any third party could have told them what was obvious.

"Do you think . . .?"

They stammered together, stopped, faced an awkward silence.

Michael frowned. It was now or never. This chance meeting might not come again. What did he have to lose? But it was what he could win that made him take the gamble.

"Would you be willing to try it again, Raf?"

That was all he could manage, though there was so much more to say. How empty his life was, how badly he missed her, what if and if only.

It was enough. She could read between the lines.

"We must make it different this time," she urged.

"We will," he said.

Raffie's arms encircled her lover as she climbed on the cycle. Both sat still to savour the moment, two halves joining back together. Then they drove off, their bodies erect on the vehicle like a victory sign waved in the face of Fate.

They come to a crossroads in a high place that overlooks the green hills of their land. A wind gusts from the sea beyond. He furls his great cloak around her, draws her close. They look into each other's eyes where the universe shines.

"The curse has been broken. We are free at last, my Lady."

She smiles at him with the amiable impassivity of the gods.

"Shall we walk on into the night, Beloved? Or will we turn to stone and watch the sky forever?"

Fiction is more bearable than reality and beyond that, better still, the dream. I continue to believe. In magic. In love. The only tragedy is despair.